Nate gazed ... *multicolore...* ...*...stmas tree.*

Her sweep of blond hair reflected sparkles of red and gold and purple. All those tender emotions he had fought so hard against returned stronger than ever and he couldn't help himself. He stepped forward and lowered his mouth to hers.

She sighed his name as he kissed her, and her arms slid around his neck.

Now. *Now* the night felt perfect. Their kiss was slow and easy, like sinking into a soft bed at the end of a hard day.

Her mouth made him crazy. He thought he could spend forever just exploring every inch of those lips. He pulled her closer while the fire hummed and sparked behind them.

He wanted Emery Kendall more than all the Christmas presents he had ever wanted in his life put together.

Dear Reader,

Being a writer is a magical thing. What a marvelous opportunity—to be able to create people out of only my imagination. By the time I've finished a book, my characters always feel like real friends to me.

They become people I care about, who inevitably have a lasting impact in my life. That's why it was such a delight to revisit the Dalton family in *A Cold Creek Holiday*. I've written other books set in Cold Creek and have had characters of previous books make guest appearances occasionally, but never to the extent of this story. So many of my previous characters played significant roles in the story of Emery Kendall and Nate Cavazos. In a way, seeing them all again was like a warm, crazy, fun family reunion. It definitely felt like coming home.

And isn't that what the holidays are all about?

My very best to you and yours this holiday season.

RaeAnne

A COLD CREEK HOLIDAY

RAEANNE THAYNE

SPECIAL EDITION

Published by Silhouette Books

America's Publisher of Contemporary Romance

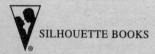

SILHOUETTE BOOKS

Recycling programs
for this product may
not exist in your area.

ISBN-13: 978-0-373-65495-6

A COLD CREEK HOLIDAY

Copyright © 2009 by RaeAnne Thayne

Visit Silhouette Books at www.eHarlequin.com

Printed in U.S.A.

Books by RaeAnne Thayne

RAEANNE THAYNE

finds inspiration in the beautiful northern Utah mountains, where she lives with her husband and three children. Her books have won numerous honors, including three RITA® Award nominations from Romance Writers of America and a Career Achievement Award from *RT Book Reviews* magazine. RaeAnne loves to hear from readers and can be reached through her Web site at www.raeannethayne.com.

To Elden and RaNae Robinson, my parents,
for fifty wonderful years together. I love you!

Chapter One

Few things gave a woman a sense of her own vulnerability like driving on an unfamiliar mountain road in the dark through a snowstorm.

Her knuckles white on the wheel of the small SUV she had rented at the Jackson Hole Airport, Emery Kendall squinted through the blowing flakes the wipers tried to beat away, desperate for any sign she was even on the right road.

The GPS unit on the rental wasn't working—naturally—and the directions she had printed off the Internet had already proved fallible twice.

She let out a breath. Stupid. This whole thing was a colossal mistake. What had seemed like such a logical plan in September, even a welcome excuse to escape the weight of her pain and grief and memories during the holidays, had lost a great deal of its allure the first time her tires slipped in the two or three inches of unplowed snow and the vehicle slid toward the ominous stretch of river ribboning beside the canyon road.

She had every reason to hate driving in the snow. It brought back too much pain, too many memories, and she couldn't help asking herself what on earth she was doing here. She should be safe at home in Virginia, snug in her townhouse with a fire crackling in the grate and a mug of hot cocoa at her elbow while she tried to wrap her recalcitrant head around her latest project.

Alone.

She clicked the wipers up to a faster rhythm as she approached a slight break in the dark silhouette of trees lining either side of the road.

A log arch over the side road was barely visible in her headlights, but she saw enough to make out the words burned into the wood.

Hope Springs Guest Ranch. Finally.

The owners really ought to think about a few well-placed landscaping lights so weary travelers knew they were in the right place.

Not that it was any of her business how they ran their guest ranch. Right now the only thing she cared about was reaching her rented cabin, hauling her things inside and collapsing on the bed for the next two or three days.

She turned into the driveway, which was unplowed with no tracks indicating anyone else had driven this way recently, at least not since the snow started to fall.

As the tires of the four-wheel-drive whirred through the virgin powder, that sense of vulnerability and unease returned, not so much from the weather now as the sobering realization that she was heading alone to a strange place—and, she had to admit, from the knowledge that the

Cold Creek Land & Cattle Company was only a mile or so up the road.

The Daltons. Three men, brothers. Wade, Jake and Seth.

A tangle of conflicting emotions tumbled through her, but she quickly pushed them all away, as she had been doing since the September night when her mother's dying confession had rocked the entire foundation of her world.

Not now. All that could wait. At the moment, the more pressing need was to get out of this snow before she became hopelessly stranded and ended up freezing to death in a snow bank on the side of some obscure mountain road.

No Christmas lights illuminated the night, which she found odd for a guest ranch. Even a little string of white lights along the fenceline would have provided a much more cheery welcome than the unrelenting darkness.

Just when she was wondering if she had imagined that sign out front, she reached a cluster of buildings. A white-painted barn and a two-story log home dominated the scene and she was relieved to see the house ablaze with light.

The woman she had spoken with when she made the reservation months ago told her to check in at the main house. She had confirmed her reservation a few weeks ago and received the same instructions, though this time from a rather flighty sounding girl who had been somewhat vague, even as she assured Emery everything was in order for her arrival.

A cold wind dug under her jacket as she walked up the steps to the wide front porch, and she was grateful for her wool scarf and hat.

She rang the bell beside a carved wooden door and a few seconds later she heard from inside the thud of running feet and a decidedly young female voice. "Doorbell! Somebody's here! I'll get it, Uncle Nate."

Three heartbeats later, the door swung open and a dark-eyed girl of perhaps seven or eight peered out.

She didn't say anything, didn't even smile, just simply gazed out in her blue thermal pajamas, as if finding a bedraggled traveler on their doorstep in the middle of a stormy December night was a daily occurrence.

She supposed it likely was. They did run a guest ranch, after all.

Despite the girl's impassive expression, Emery forced a smile. "Hi. I'm Emery Kendall. I think I'm expected. I'm sorry I'm so late."

"It's okay. We're not in bed yet. Just a minute." She shifted her head and called over her shoulder. "Uncle Nate. It's a lady in a really pretty hat."

Emery touched her cloche, one of her own creations.

The girl held the door wide-open, but Emery didn't feel quite right about walking inside, invited only by an eight-year-old. Conversely, she also didn't feel right about standing in the open doorway, allowing all the delicious warmth from inside to wash past her and dissipate in the storm.

Before she could make up her mind, a man in a dark green wool henley, flannel shirt and Levi's walked into the entry.

He exuded danger, from his hard eyes to his unsmiling mouth to the solid, unyielding set to his jaw.

She had that unsettling cognizance of her own vulnerability again. Who knew she was coming to Idaho? Only Lulu, the manager of her store, and Freddie, her best friend.

Solitary Traveler Shows Up at Dark Mountain Lodge in a Storm, Never to Be Heard from Again. She could just see the headline now.

Or maybe she had spent too many sleepless nights in the past two years watching old Alfred Hitchcock movies on the classic film channel.

Just because the man *looked* dangerous didn't mean he necessarily was. How many serial killers sent little girls who called them Uncle Nate to greet their victims?

"Yes?" he asked, in a decidedly unwelcoming tone.

"I'm Emery Kendall."

He met her gaze with raised eyebrows and a blank look. "Sorry, is that supposed to mean something to me?"

If not for that sign out front, she would have worried she had the wrong place. Now she just wondered what wires had been crossed about her arrival date.

Either that, or this was the most inhospitable guest lodge it had ever been her misfortune to find.

"I have a reservation to stay in one of your cabins until the twenty-seventh of December," she said, fighting down that unease again. "I made the initial reservation several months ago and confirmed it only a few weeks ago with a woman named Joanie something or other. I have the paperwork if you'd like to confirm it."

"Joanie ran off." The pajama-clad girl had followed the man back into the room and she spoke in a matter-of-fact tone. "Uncle Nate is really mad."

"Uncle Nate" did indeed look upset. His mouth tightened even more and his eyes darkened to a hard black. She felt an unexpected pang of sympathy for the unknown woman. She wouldn't like to have all that leashed frustration aimed in *her* direction.

"Damn fool woman," he muttered.

For one crazy moment, she thought he meant her, then realized he must be referring to the absent Joanie.

"Is there a problem?" She couldn't help stating the obvious.

"You might say that." He raked a hand through short dark hair. "We run a pretty low-key operation here, Ms. Kendall. This isn't your average five-star hotel. We've only got a few guest cabins that are mostly empty in the winter."

"I understood that completely when I made the reservation. I saw the Web site and reviews and talked at length about the amenities with the woman who initially took my reservation. I'm perfectly fine with the arrangements."

She didn't add that they were ideal for her purposes, to be left alone for the holidays, away from the gaiety and the frenzy and the memories.

Not to mention the proximity of Hope Springs Guest Ranch to the Cold Creek ranch.

"Yeah, well, we've got one employee who usually handles everything from reservations to making the beds. Joanie Reynolds."

"And?"

"And three days ago, she ran off with a cowboy she met at the Million Dollar Bar and I haven't seen her since. You want the truth, we're in a hell of a mess."

He didn't look apologetic in the slightest, only frustrated, as if the whole mess were *Emery's* fault.

She was exhausted suddenly from the long day of traveling, from flight delays and long security lines and two hours of driving on unfamiliar roads. All she wanted was to sink into a bed somewhere and sleep until she could think straight once more.

"What do you suggest I do, then? I had a reservation. I made a deposit and everything. And I've been traveling for eight hours."

She heard the slightly forlorn note in her voice and wanted to wince. Nate Whoever-He-Was must have heard it, too. A trace of regret flickered in the depths of those dangerous dark eyes.

He sighed heavily. "Come in out of the cold. We'll figure something out."

She hesitated for just a moment, that serial-killer scenario flitting through her head again, but she pushed it away. Little girl, remember?

Inside the house, she was immediately struck by the vague sense of neglect. The furnishings were warm and comfortable, an appealing mix of antique, reproduction and folk art pieces. Through the doorway, she glimpsed a great room with soaring vaulted ceilings. A lovely old schoolhouse quilt had prominence against the wall and she fought the urge to whip out her sketchbook and pencils to get those particular umber and moss tones down on paper.

But she also didn't miss the cobwebs in the corner of the space and a messy pile of mail and unread newspapers scattered across the top of the console table in the entryway where she stood.

Nor did she miss the wide, muscled shoulders of the man, or the way they tapered to slim hips.

"Is there anywhere else close by I could stay?" she asked, more than a little aghast at her inconvenient and unexpected reaction to him.

He turned with a frown and she sincerely hoped he couldn't see that little niggle of attraction.

"Not really, I'm sorry to say," he answered. "There are a couple other guest ranches in the area, but everybody else closes down for the winter. There's a motel in town, but I couldn't recommend it."

"Why do you stay open when everybody else shuts down?"

He made a face as if the very question had occurred to him more than once. "We have some hardcore snowmobilers who've been staying since the ranch opened to guests five years ago. Their bookings are being honored, though we haven't taken new ones since…well, probably since you made your reservations."

A muscle flexed in his jaw. "Look, do you mind waiting here while I check the computer?"

"I have a copy of my reservation in the rental. I can get it for you."

"I believe you. I just want to figure out what Joanie has done. For all I know, we're hosting a damn convention she forgot to mention to me before she ran off. Just give me five minutes."

He walked away, leaving her standing in the entryway with the little girl—who was suddenly joined by another girl who looked perhaps a few years older. Her hair wasn't quite as long and her features were thinner. But just like her sister—they looked so much alike, they could be nothing else—she said nothing, just regarded Emery with solemn, dark eyes.

Something strange was going on at the Hope Springs Ranch. She couldn't help noticing a large artificial Christmas tree in the great room, but it was bare of lights or ornaments, and as far as she could tell, that was the only concession to the holidays within her view.

"I really like your hat," the younger girl who had answered the door finally said to break the silence.

She smiled at her, despite her exhaustion. "Thank you. I made it."

"You made it?" The older girl's eyes widened. "Like you sewed it and stuff?"

"Yes. And I designed the material."

The girl frowned, clearly skeptical. "Nobody designs material. You just buy it at the sewing store. That's what our mom used to do anyway."

"Before she died," the younger one added.

"Be quiet, Tallie," her sister snapped. "She doesn't need to know *everything*."

Emery wanted to tell them she might not know everything, but she did know about losing a mother. Her own had only been gone a few months. But she supposed the experience of a twenty-seven-year-old woman losing her mother was quite different than that of two young girls.

"You do pick out material in a fabric store," she answered. "But someone has to design the material in the first place and decide what color dyes and what sort of fibers to use. That's what I do."

She didn't add that her fledgling textile line had recently been called "innovative, exciting and warmly elegant" by the leading trade magazine.

"Can you show me how to make a hat like that?"

"Me, too!" The younger girl exclaimed. "If Claire gets to make one, I want to. I can give it to my friend Frances for Christmas."

"Ooh, maybe I could make two," her sister said. "One for Natalie and one for Morgan. They're my very best friends."

"Can I make a pink one?" Tallie asked. "I *love* pink, and so does Frances."

"Ooh, I would like purple," her sister said. "Or maybe red."

Emery shifted, wondering where in Hades their uncle had disappeared to and how the situation had suddenly spiraled out of her control. It must be the fatigue—or perhaps her complete lack of experience with young girls.

"I don't even know if I'm staying here yet. Your uncle and I are still working out the details."

The expression on both faces shifted from excitement to resignation in a blink and she wondered what in their young lives had contributed to their cynicism.

She hated sounding like such a grump, especially toward two girls who had lost their mother. "If I'm staying, we can see," she amended.

That was apparently enough for them. For the next few moments the girls talked about colors and patterns until their uncle returned to the room.

"Your reservation wasn't on the main calendar in the office, but I found it on a deleted copy of her files from the hard drive backup. I don't know what happened. Everything is in such a mess."

"Is the cabin I reserved available, then?"

He sighed. "Nobody else is staying there, so I suppose you could say it's available. But Joanie basically ran the lodging side of things and I haven't had time to replace her yet. I'm going to have to scramble just to find maid service. It might take me a few days, so you might want to reconsider and find a place in Jackson Hole. We'll of course fully refund your deposit."

"I don't need maid service. I can take care of myself. I just need a quiet place where I can get some work done."

He studied her for a long moment then finally shrugged. "I think you're crazy, but what do I know? If you want to stay, I suppose it wouldn't be fair of me to turn you away since you've had a reservation for several months. Let me grab my coat and I'll take you down and open the cabin."

"Yay! You're staying." Tallie beamed at her as Nate reached into a closet in the hallway and emerged with fleece-lined ranch coat. "Now you can show us how to make a hat."

"She only said we could see," the older girl warned her sister. "That usually means no."

"Ms. Kendall is our guest," their uncle said with what she was beginning to consider his characteristic frown. "You girls are not to pester her. You know the rules."

Though Emery had been seeking a tactful way to discourage them, she had a sudden obstinate urge to do exactly the opposite.

"Give me a day or two to settle in. I brought my sewing machine and some fabric samples we could probably use."

"Who packs a sewing machine for a holiday visit to the mountains?"

She forced a smile. "I'm not here to ski, Mr...."

"Sorry. Cavazos. Nate Cavazos."

"Mr. Cavazos. This is a working vacation for me. I just need peace and quiet to finish several projects awaiting my attention. The setting doesn't really matter."

That was an outright lie, but she decided it was none of Nate Cavavos's business exactly why she had come to Cold Creek.

Damn tourists.

Nate grabbed the key to the biggest and best of the four small cabins his sister and her husband had built along Cold Creek.

If he had his way, he would send Miss Fancy Kendall back to Jackson Hole, just be blunt and tell her in no uncertain terms that there was no room at the inn.

What the hell did he know about running a guest ranch? He was a highly trained military specialist with a background in explosives. He knew about blowing things up and planning clandestine operations. Organized chaos was his specialty, not fluffing pillows and fetching tea for sleek city women who drove Lexus SUVs and looked as if they just stepped out of some après skiwear catalog.

Damn the woman and damn Joanie Reynolds for running off and leaving such a mess behind.

"If you'll follow me, you can park your vehicle next to the cabin. I'll unlock it for you and make sure the heat's working, then help you with your bags."

"That's not necessary, really. Both of us don't need to go out into the storm. I can take the key and let myself in if you'll just point me in the right direction."

He ignored her and opened the door. "Claire, keep an eye on Tallie for me, okay? I'll be back in a minute. I've got my cell with me if you need me."

"Okay."

She was too agreeable, his oldest niece. He hadn't seen her a great deal in her eleven years, just the occasional visit between deployments, but he remembered her as always being eager to please. In the three months since her parents died, she had become even more so, though she still tried to boss her younger sister around as if she were trying desperately to control that one little corner of a chaotic universe.

"When can we make the hats?" Tallie asked.

"What hats?"

Emery Kendall pointed to hers. "They were admiring my cloche. I told them I could perhaps help them sew one of their own."

He didn't know what the hell a cloche was. It sounded

French and vaguely sexy, especially to a man who hadn't been with a woman since before his last tour of duty.

"Girls, you're not to bother our guests. You know that."

"They weren't bothering me," she protested. "I told them we could see in a few days, once I settle in."

His mouth tightened. That was the *last* thing he needed, for his grieving, emotionally hungry nieces to suddenly decide to latch onto this stranger who was only going to be here for a week or so.

They missed their mother and father terribly. The hell of it was, he had come to the conclusion he was far worse at parenting than he was at running a guest ranch.

"You don't have entertain Tallie and Claire," he said, his voice gruff. "Especially when you've got work of your own to do."

She looked as if she wanted to argue, but he wasn't at all in the mood to tangle with her anymore tonight. He wanted to get the blasted woman settled in to her cabin and come back to the house so he could figure out where the hell his life had gone so disastrously off-track in a few short months.

"You girls go on up to bed," he said. Though it was an order, he tried not to phrase it as such. He had learned the first few weeks after Suzi and John died that eight- and eleven-year-old girls didn't respond like trained commandos to terse commands. "I'll check on you when I come back inside."

Without waiting for their answer—or to see if Ms. Kendall followed him—he turned up his collar, pulled down his Stetson and headed out into the lightly blowing snow.

He was halfway down the driveway he hadn't had time to plow yet and trudging toward the cabins a few hundred yards away from the house before he heard her vehicle start up behind him.

He had to admit, his sister and her husband had picked a good spot for guest cabins. When he was a kid, this part of the struggling ranch had held rusting old farm equipment and a ramshackle shed or two. But Suzi and John had cleared all that out and built four comfortable log cabins out of old salvaged timbers and white chinking so they looked as if they had been there forever.

In the daylight, the place had a nice view of the west slope of the Tetons and of Cold Creek Canyon. And Suzi had made the inside of each cabin warm and welcoming.

He didn't know much about this sort of thing. As long as he had a sleeping bag and a tight-weave tent to keep out the worst of the bugs and the sandstorms, he was fine. But he imagined the guests of the ranch Suzi had renamed Hope Springs probably appreciated the handmade curtains and the lodgepole pine furnishings.

He unlocked the first cabin and immediately switched on the electric fireplace in the main room and the smaller fireplace in the bedroom. Between the two of them, they did a surprisingly effective job of keeping the place toasty in only a matter of minutes.

He walked back out onto the porch and found the blasted woman trying to wrestle a huge suitcase out of the cargo space of the SUV.

"I said I'd help you with your bags," he muttered.

Despite the dim light from the porch and the swirl of snow, he didn't miss the cool look she sent him out of lovely blue eyes he didn't want to notice.

"I appreciate your…courtesy."

He didn't miss the slight, subtle pause before she said

the last word. Though he wanted to bark and growl and tell her where to shove that delicate hint of sarcasm, he forced a tight smile.

"Here at Hope Springs, we're nothing if not courteous," he said in a benign sort of voice that matched her own.

He reached down and pulled the suitcase away from her then lifted another one out. The back was chock-full with five suitcases and several bags of groceries. At least Joanie must have had the foresight despite her typical ditziness to encourage their guest to shop for food before she arrived. He was grateful for that, at least. The ranch didn't provide any meals and the nearest restaurant was six miles down the canyon in Pine Gulch, but the cabin was outfitted with a full kitchen.

Between the two of them, it only took a few trips to empty out the back of her vehicle and set everything inside the now-toasty cabin.

When he returned inside with the last load, he found her in the kitchen, putting away food from the grocery bags.

She had taken off her coat and beneath it she wore a pale blue turtleneck that showed just how nicely curved she was in all the right places.

He didn't want to notice. "The kitchen should have everything you need in the way of pots and pans and that sort of thing. If you're missing anything you need, you can call up to the main house."

"I'm sure I'll be fine."

"The reservation said you're staying until the twenty-seventh. Is anyone else joining you?"

He wondered if he imagined the way she tilted her chin in a rather defiant sort of way. "No."

She was staying here by herself through Christmas? He

wasn't big on celebrating the holidays himself, but he had to wonder what would make a soft, pretty woman like Emery Kendall leave everything familiar and hide out in the Idaho wilderness alone during Christmas.

None of his business, he reminded himself. He had enough on his plate without spending a minute wondering why she wanted to hole up here by herself.

"If you need anything, the number to the main house is the top button programmed on the phone," he said.

"I'm sure I'll be fine. Thank you for your help." She paused. "Actually, there is one thing. When I made the initial reservation, I was told I was welcome to use any of the Hope Springs horses during my stay."

"That's generally the policy. If you need help saddling a horse, you can usually find me or Bill Higgins, the hired man, somewhere around the place."

"I shouldn't need help. I've been around horses most of my life. But thank you."

A woman who sewed fancy hats, wore her clothes with the kind of flair that belonged in a fashion magazine, drove a rented Lexus SUV and apparently had plenty of experience with horses. He gave a mental head shake as he said good-night and walked back into the December night.

He wasn't sure what to think of her. Nothing, he reminded himself. He didn't need to spend one more minute than necessary thinking about the woman. She was a guest at the ranch, that was all. One he would be thrilled to send on her way at the earliest possible opportunity.

Chapter Two

She slept better than she had in months.

It was an unexpected boon. She had never been able to sleep well in a strange bed. Coupled with the insomnia that had troubled her since before her mother died, Emery had anticipated a rough night.

Perhaps she had only been exhausted from the long day of travel and the complications of her arrival. Whatever the reason for her deep sleep, she awoke invigorated, her mind racing with ideas for the boutique hotel redesign she was working on for one of her favorite clients, Spencer Hotels.

This is exactly what she hoped might happen, that escaping from her routine in Warrenton might help her recapture some of the joy she had always found when a new project started to click in her head.

What she had taken to be a blizzard the night before left only about three or four inches of new snow on the ground.

She opened the rather ordinary beige tab curtains to the alpine scene outside her windows and spent the morning with her sketchbook.

The hotel Eben Spencer had recently purchased was in Livingston, Montana, gateway to the north entrance of Yellowstone. He wanted mountain chic with an edge and custom everything—window coverings, upholstery, bed linens.

By early afternoon, she had filled her sketchbook with several possibilities she thought would work for the property. After a quick bowl of canned tomato soup and half a sandwich, the lure of the brilliant blue sky—the pure clarity of it against the dark green pine topped with snow—was too powerful for her to resist.

She bundled into silk long johns and her warmest outdoor gear and decided to check out the ranch's equine offerings.

As she walked past red-painted outbuildings toward the large horse barn and corrals she had spied the night before on her way in, she saw no sign of her reluctant host. Her only companion was a magpie who squawked at her from atop the split-rail fence then hopped away in a flash of iridescent wings.

At the horse barn, a half dozen horses munched alfalfa that had recently been spread for them in the snow-covered pasture and it appeared as if that many again preferred the warmth of the barn.

She stood at the railing, admiring the quarter horses. She could see a couple mares were ready to foal and all of them looked well-fed and content.

After a few moments, a strong-boned dappled gray gelding wandered over to her spot and dipped his head for a little love.

"You are a pretty boy, aren't you," she murmured and he whinnied and tossed his head as if in complete agreement.

"That one was our mom's horse."

She whirled around and found the girls from the night before watching her from the corner of the pasture. Claire and Tallie, she remembered.

They wore jeans and parkas and mismatched gloves and Tallie's hair was slipping out of her braid. Had her sister fixed it or had Nate? The idea of that dangerous-looking man trying to wrangle his niece's hair tugged at her emotions.

"Hi," she greeted the girls.

"That was our mom's favorite horse," Claire repeated.

"He's beautiful," Emery answered.

"His name is Cielo. It means *cloud* in Spanish," the younger girl said. "You can ride him if you want."

"Oh, I don't…"

Tallie didn't wait for her to answer. "Annabelle was our mom's other favorite horse, but she's having a baby after Christmas so you can't ride her."

"Which one is Annabelle?"

"The black with the white stockings," Claire said, gesturing to a lovely mare currently drinking from the water trough.

"So do you want to ride Cielo?"

She did, suddenly, but she was wary about riding a horse that had been a favorite of their deceased mother.

"If you're sure it's okay."

"Sure," Tallie answered, then her gamine features lit up. "Hey, she could come with us! Then we could go now."

"Where are you going?" Emery asked warily.

"Just a friend's house," Claire said.

"By yourselves?"

The girls exchanged glances. "We're allowed to ride as long as we have someone with us," Claire finally answered, an explanation Emery didn't completely buy.

"What were you planning to do before you ran into me here?"

"Wait." Tallie heaved a put-upon sigh. "We've been waiting all morning, and Uncle Nate is *still* busy with the man who came from Idaho Fall."

"The lawyer," Claire said. "He's talking about our mom and dad's state."

It took Emery a moment to deduce their uncle and the attorney must be discussing their parents' estate. Poor little things, to lose both their mother and their father.

Let that be a lesson to her. Just when she was tempted to wallow in self-pity at the strange journey her life had taken over the past few years, she was completely gobsmacked by someone whose path was even tougher.

"I'm sure they'll be finished soon."

"But we have an important mission," Tallie declared. "We can't wait much longer. We really can't."

Emery couldn't help her smile. Had she been so dramatic at eight? "What could possibly be so urgent?"

"Our friend Tanner has been home sick from school for three whole days."

Again, Emery had to swallow a smile at the gravity in the girl's voice. "Oh my goodness. I hope it's nothing serious."

"He had the flu and was throwing up and everything. He said it was really gross. But his stepmom said he's feeling tons better."

"That's a relief." Emery was surprised to find herself enjoying her interaction with these cute girls.

"Yeah, only I brought home all his homework papers

yesterday and I just *have* to get them to his house so he has time to finish them before school on Monday or he'll be in big trouble."

"I can see why you're in such a hurry, then."

"So will you come with us?" Claire asked. "We can help you saddle Cielo."

She looked at the powerful horse and then back at the girls. She had been considering a ride. And by the looks of him, riding Cielo would indeed be like riding a cloud. What would be the harm in going along with the girls and saving Nate Cavazos a little work?

"We'd better make sure it's all right with your uncle."

"I'm sure he won't mind," Claire said. "This way he doesn't have to find the time to take us."

"Why don't you ask him anyway? I would feel better if he gave his okay. Tallie and I will saddle the horses and meet you at the house in a few minutes, all right?"

Claire gave a reluctant sigh, but nodded. "Tallie, you get Junebug for me. And don't cinch her too tight."

"I know. I've only done it a million times."

Claire returned to the barn a few moments later, just as they were saddling Tallie's small paint pony, a pretty little mare she called Estrella.

"Did he say it was okay?"

"Yep," Claire said, her attention turned to her own horse.

"Good," Emery answered, surprised at how much she was anticipating a good, hard ride. "Does it take long to reach Tanner's house?"

"It's not far. Maybe a mile," Tallie answered. Before Emery could ask if she needed a hand into the saddle, the girl clambered up like a little monkey and settled easily on the horse's back.

Both girls looked completely at home in the saddle and Emery, who had been riding since she was younger than either of them, though with an English saddle, felt like a veritable greenhorn in comparison.

"Come on. Let's go," Tallie insisted, nudging the heels of her boots into the horse's side.

The younger girl led the way down the snowy driveway and both of the other horses followed Estrella with alacrity, tack jingling softly and their gaits smart, as if they were thrilled to be out in the cold, invigorating air.

The mountains loomed over them, raw and jagged, their peaks a dramatic contrast of snow and pine.

At the end of the long, curving drive, they followed the canyon road along the creek for perhaps a half mile. In that time, they encountered no vehicles.

"Are we getting closer to Tanner's house?" Emery asked after a few more moments.

"Not very far. Look, there's the sign for it."

She followed the direction of the girl's outstretched hand and her heart clutched in her chest.

A huge log arch spanned the driveway, much bigger than the sign for the Hope Springs Guest Ranch had been. This one declared Cold Creek Land & Cattle Company in black iron letters.

Oh, dear heavens.

She wasn't ready. She still hadn't decided if she would *ever* be ready. She needed more time to figure out if she wanted to face any of the Daltons yet.

She wanted to whirl Cielo around and ride as fast and as hard as she could back to the relative safety of Hope Springs.

"What's the matter, Ms. Kendall?" Tallie's mouth puckered into a concerned frown. "You look funny."

She didn't feel funny. Far from it. She felt panicked and vaguely nauseous, the canned tomato soup suddenly turning to greasy sludge in her stomach.

She drew in a breath. She could do this. The Daltons knew nothing about the revelations that had completely rocked her world four months ago. As far as they knew, she was only a guest staying at a neighboring ranch.

"Nothing." She forced a smile and eased her hands on the reins. "Nothing at all."

Her heart pounded as they rode under the arch and headed up a long driveway that wound around a stand of lodgepole pine and bare-branched aspens.

The house was a grand, imposing log structure with a long front porch and several gables, surrounded by several outbuildings. Some distance from it, she could see a large, sprawling metal-framed building. She guessed that was the Cold Creek equine training facility she had read about on the Internet.

Her heart felt as if it would pound right out of her chest and she couldn't seem to catch her breath in the cold air. She hadn't had a panic attack since she graduated from college, not even during the worst of her pain and loss during the past two years, and she really didn't want to start again.

Breathe, she ordered herself.

When they neared the house, the girls jumped down from their horses and Emery knew she couldn't go inside.

"I'll just wait for you out here with the horses," she told them. "You go give your friend his homework."

The implications of the connection began to sink through. Tanner must be one of the Dalton children. Wade's, probably, since as far as she could determine, he was the only brother with grade-school-age kids, although Seth had older stepchildren. That made Tallie's friend Tanner her…

She jerked her mind away. "Go ahead. I'll be fine."

"Okay, but we might be a few minutes. You might get cold. I told Tanner I would explain our math assignment to him and I don't know how long it will take."

Before she could come up with an answer, a tall, dark-haired man with a definite air of authority walked out of a nearby barn. He stopped short when he spied them, then his handsome features lit up.

"Well, hello there, Miss Tallie and Miss Claire," he called as he approached them. "What brings you all the way up to the Cold Creek on such a wintry day?"

Emery drew in a calming breath and then another one. He looked just like the picture she had of his father. Which brother was it? Her guess was Wade. He ran the family's cattle operations, from what she could determine, while the youngest brother, Seth, was in charge of the horse training facility. A third brother, Jake, was a family physician in Pine Gulch.

She could have hired a private investigator to find all this information, but she hadn't needed to go that far. A few clicks on the computer and she had found all she needed to know and then some.

"I've got Tanner's homework, Mr. Dalton."

"That is sure nice of you girls to ride over for that. It will give him something to do besides snipe at his brother and sister. He'll be real glad to see a little company. And who's your friend?"

"Her name is Ms. Kendall and she's from Virginia," Claire answered.

Emery didn't feel she had any choice but to dismount. She prayed her shaking legs would hold her up.

"I'm Emery Kendall. I'm staying at Hope Springs through the holidays."

He wore a battered leather work glove, but he removed it and reached out his hand. She shook it then quickly dropped her fingers.

"Nice to meet you, Miz Kendall. You picked a beautiful time of year for a visit. This area of eastern Idaho is pretty year round, but there's something special about the place during the holidays, as long as you can stand the cold."

She had only seen the one picture, but she knew his father shared that same smile, that same thick, wavy, dark hair.

"Let's tie your horses so you can come in out of the cold for a minute and I'll let Tanner know you all are here," he said. "And don't worry, he's not contagious anymore. Just grumpy as can be."

The girls giggled at that and followed him back up the porch steps and into the house.

The house was huge and warm and welcoming. Here were the Christmas decorations the girls' home lacked. A massive Christmas tree decorated with plaid ribbons and hundreds of ornaments brushed the top of the soaring vaulted ceiling and pine garlands with matching ribbons draped the river rock fireplace and hung from the log staircase.

Whoever decorated the place had used a pleasing mix of color and texture to create a sense of brightness and warmth.

She was studying a particularly lovely embroidered sampler on the wall when a woman with blond hair and fine-boned features entered the room.

"Tallie and Claire Palmer. Two of my favorite people!"

"We brought Tanner's homework assignment. Mrs. Peterson said he can turn it in when he goes back to class."

"He'll be so excited to see you," the woman said with a warm smile. "Come on back to the kitchen. I just took a tray of cookies out of the oven. You'd better come grab one before the hungry little mouths around here gobble them all up."

"And the hungry big mouths."

The man owning the hungry big mouth in question swooped the woman into his arms and planted it on hers and kissed her soundly, apparently unembarrassed by the presence of a stranger.

"You'll have to fight Cody for them, I'm afraid," she answered after he released her. "He's already snitched three off the cookie sheet before I could even transfer them to the cooling rack. I'm sure he had to have burned his tongue, but he'll never admit it."

Wade Dalton chuckled, then apparently remembered his manners. "Sorry. Carrie, this is Emery Kendall. She's staying at Hope Springs and was nice enough to ride with the girls over here to bring Tanner's homework. Emery, this is my wife, Caroline. If you'll excuse me, I'm going to go fight off my kids for the cookies. It was nice to meet you."

"Thank you," she murmured. Only after he left the room did her heart rate seem to settle down.

"Tanner and Nat are in the family room playing video games," Caroline said to the girls. "I'm sure Tanner would love some company besides family for a few minutes if you've got time to visit."

The girls looked to Emery as if for permission and she wasn't quite sure how to respond. Right now she didn't feel in charge of anything, not even her own breathing. "A few moments, I suppose. Then we'd better ride back before your uncle begins to worry."

"I told Tanner I would explain the math assignment," Tallie said. "We're subtracting fractions and stuff and it's really hard."

"That is so kind of you to help him," Caroline said with a warm smile. "I don't know what we would have done without you."

Though it was only a first impression and she could be way off-base, for all she knew, Emery thought the other woman seemed completely sincere in her gratitude, the sort of person who could lift even the most defeated spirit just with her smile.

She would have been very much inclined to like her, even if she hadn't already read and admired Caroline Montgomery Dalton's self-help books on finding your life's direction before she knew of the connection to the Daltons of Cold Creek Canyon.

"Emery, where did you say you were from?" Caroline asked when the girls hurried from the room.

"Virginia. Warrenton, an hour outside Washington, D.C."

"Lovely country there. Are you in Pine Gulch visiting family?" Caroline asked.

Under the circumstances, Emery didn't quite know how to respond to that particular question.

"I guess you could say I needed a change this Christmas. It's been a…difficult year. My mother died of cancer in September."

"Oh, I'm so sorry for your loss. I can only imagine how hard the holidays must be for you."

Though she didn't physically touch her, the concern in her voice was somehow just as comforting as an embrace.

"The grief is still very painful, especially as she was my…only family. I wasn't quite ready to face the parties and celebrations of the holidays and was looking for a change this year. I read about Hope Springs Guest Ranch online and it seemed just the place to spend the holidays."

"It's a very peaceful spot," Caroline said softly. "I've always thought it had healing energy. I know Suzi, the girls' mother, felt the same."

She didn't expect to find healing. She only wanted to figure out how everything she thought she had known about herself could turn out to be a lie.

"I'm surprised Nate is taking new guests. I was under the impression he's working toward closing the place, which is really a shame after all the work and heart and soul Suzi and John put into it."

"I made my reservation back in September. There was some mix-up with it, but Mr. Cavazos agreed to honor it."

"He has his hands full, that man."

Before Emery could answer, a timer dinged from somewhere in the house. Caroline glanced behind her.

"My cookies are just coming out. Listen, do you mind coming back to the kitchen with me? I don't want to leave you out here by yourself, but if I don't take them out, they'll burn. Of course, they'll still get inhaled around here, no matter how crispy they are."

"I don't mind," she answered. She followed Caroline down a hallway toward the origin of the delicious smells of almond and butter and sugar. The hallway was lined with photographs, old black-and-whites, framed snapshots and some that looked like professionally taken portraits. Emery's head swiveled as she took in the barrage of images and she had to stop so she could absorb them all.

"This is…your family?"

"Yes." She noticed the direction of Emery's gaze, a candid shot of three men in Western-cut suits standing at what looked like a wedding. They were laughing and light-hearted, each of them extraordinarily handsome. "Those are my husband's brothers, Jake and Seth. That was taken at Seth's wedding. They both live nearby, which is wonderful for all of them. We're very close with them and their wives."

She couldn't stand here gaping at someone else's family, not without making Caroline Montgomery Dalton think she was crazy, so she followed her down the hallway into the kitchen, doing her best not to cast longing looks over her shoulder.

In the kitchen, she found Wade Dalton sitting at a long, scarred pine table with a blonde toddler in pink overalls on his lap and a little boy of about five or six chattering a mile a minute at his side.

"I got to help make the holes for the jam, Dad. Only even though they're called thumbprint cookies, Mom wouldn't let me use my thumbs to make the dents. I had to use the lid of a marker. Don't you think that's weird?"

"Extremely," he answered with a grin toward Emery and Caroline. "But probably a little more sanitary."

"There's a method to my madness," Caroline said. "That way the jam doesn't ooze out the sides as easily. It's all in how much pressure you apply when you make the hole, isn't it, bud?"

The boy nodded emphatically. "And I'm just right, aren't I?"

"You're perfect."

Emery stood aside, observing their interaction while Caroline pulled the cookies from the oven in one smooth motion and replaced that tray with another filled with dough cutouts.

When she had set them on a cooling rack, she turned back to Emery. "So what do you do in Virginia, Emery?"

"I design textiles. I've got a shop outside D.C. that sells custom fabrics for interior designers, furniture makers, that sort of thing. We're moving into the retail market in the fall with a new midrange consumer line."

"How interesting," Caroline exclaimed. "I wish I could sew, but I'm afraid it's not one of my skills. How did you get started in that particular business? It seems rather obscure."

Emery knew from her research that Caroline Montgomery Dalton was a life coach who probably excelled at convincing people to talk about their hopes and dreams, but she was still flattered by the woman's interested expression. "I waffled between graphic arts and interior design in college, but realized my real love was creating at the sewing machine. After I interned with one of the bigger textile design firms, I decided to branch out in my own direction."

"I'd love to see some of your fabrics while you're here. Did you bring any swatches?"

She laughed. "Only about four boxes' worth. This is sort of a working vacation for me. I'm working on a design project for a hotel in Montana that wants custom fabrics from the ground up."

"I just had a great idea." Caroline said suddenly. "You should come to the party we're having next week."

Emery blinked, astounded that the woman would invite a perfect stranger who was only in the area temporarily to socialize with them. "What kind of party?"

"A friend and I are throwing sort of a celebration for the neighbors in Cold Creek Canyon. Everyone in the canyon is invited. Even though you're only here temporarily, that means you."

"You and a friend are throwing it," Wade said, a little dimple teasing at his cheek. "Except it's at Jenna's house and she's doing all the cooking."

"I'm helping!" Caroline protested. "I sent out all the invitations and I'm making cookies to take. Anyway, we capitalize on our strengths, right? Can I help it if she has a huge house with an indoor swimming pool and just happens to be a gourmet cook?"

Wade grinned and picked up one of the warm cookies. His mouth widened in appreciation as he bit into the soft treat. "You can take her down, honey. At least when it comes to your thumbprints."

"I'll make sure to tell her you said so, especially when you're going to town on those magic bars she makes that you love so much."

She turned back to Emery. "Seriously, it's going to be a blast. All the neighbors from Cold Creek Canyon are invited. We would love to have you. I hate the idea of anyone spending the holidays alone."

Oh, sign her up to go to a party where the only reason she had been invited was because everyone felt sorry for her. That was a big part of the reason she had opted to leave Virginia this year, so her friends wouldn't feel obligated to invite her to their own holiday gatherings out of pity.

On the other hand, Caroline was offering her the perfect opportunity to spend a little time with the Daltons in a social situation. She hadn't specifically said Wade's brothers were attending, but Emery knew from her research that they both lived in the canyon, Seth in his own home here at the ranch and Jake a bit closer to town. Besides that,

Caroline said the brothers were close so she would guess they would all attend the party.

"I'll think about it," she finally said.

"Wonderful. Nate and the girls are invited, of course, but I haven't heard from him. Maybe you could work on persuading him."

As if she could convince the man of anything. In the few moments she had spent with him the night before, he hadn't made it a secret that he wasn't exactly thrilled to have her staying at the ranch in the first place. She had a feeling he wouldn't respond favorably if she tried to manage his social life while she was there.

She was spared from having to come up with a polite answer by the arrival of Tallie and Claire, in company with a blond boy in sweats and a Utah Jazz sweatshirt—and with a definite gleam of mischief in his eyes.

"Get the homework situation straightened out?" Wade asked them.

"I guess," the boy muttered, his expression disgruntled. "I still say it's not fair I have to do homework when I'm sick."

"If you feel well enough to play video games, you can do homework," Caroline said, her voice firm even as she held out a cookie for the boy.

The girls chatted for a few more moments with Caroline and Wade and it was obvious to Emery that they were no strangers to the kitchen. She let them visit for a while while she tried not to steal surreptitious glances at Wade. Finally, though, she was afraid her not-so-subtle interest would become too obvious. She glanced at her watch, then interjected into a break in the conversation.

"We'd better start heading back."

"Do we have to?" Tallie moaned.

"Your uncle will be looking for us," she answered, though in truth, she was just as reluctant to leave. She wanted to sit here awhile longer enjoying the warmth of this family and the tensile connection to old secrets.

Tallie gave a few more put-upon sighs, but Claire only looked disappointed for a moment, then she rose. "Come on, Tal. Let's go."

"Thanks again for bringing the homework," Wade said to the girls, then turned to Emery. "It was nice to meet you."

Somehow she managed to smile back over the renewed pounding of her heart. Would he say that if he knew the truth? She had to wonder. As she ushered the girls toward the door, Caroline and Tanner followed them. On the porch, she held out two lunch bags Emery hadn't even noticed she had been carrying.

"What's this?" Emery asked.

"Cookies, a bag for you and one for Nate and the girls. And just in case I didn't mention it, they're made with jam from our own raspberry canes in the garden. I don't have very many specialties so I'm pretty proud of this one."

Caroline hugged both Tallie and Claire goodbye, sympathy in her eyes for the two little girls. To her surprise, she hugged Emery, too.

"It was great to meet you. I really would love to see some of your fabrics."

She didn't know what to do with all this warmth, especially when some insane part of her wanted to sit right down on the porch and tell Caroline Dalton everything.

"I'll see what I can do," she answered, then she and the girls headed off the porch, mounted their horses and took off down the driveway toward Hope Springs.

Chapter Three

They were all mostly silent on the way home. Emery was lost in thought, wondering if this whole trip had been crazy. What place could she ever have in the Daltons' lives? As much as she had instinctively liked both Wade and Caroline Dalton and despite the ties they didn't even know about, she was a stranger to them. What right did she have to burst into their lives, dredging up the past?

She was so wrapped up in her thoughts, she didn't pay much attention to anything until they turned onto the Hope Springs access road. As Cielo moved alongside Claire's horse, she had the first clear view of the girl in several moments and she was stunned to see silent tears trickling down cheeks reddened by the cold.

The sight jerked her from her own self-absorption and she nudged the horse closer so she could reach out to touch the girl's shoulder. "Oh, honey, what is it?"

"Nothing," Claire sniffled.

"It's the cookies Tanner's mom made," Tallie said. She looked close to tears, as well, though she seemed to be holding them back.

"What's wrong with the cookies?"

"Nothing," Claire said. "It's just…we haven't made any this year. Not real ones, anyway."

"Our mom always made Christmas cookies with us. Every year. It was so fun," Tallie said sadly.

"We made sugar cookies and wedding balls and almond ones dipped in chocolate," Claire said, her voice breaking on the words. "I miss them so much."

She let out a sob and Emery stopped her horse and pulled the girl into as much of a hug as she could manage when they were both on horseback.

"We made cookies with Uncle Nate," Tallie reminded her sister. "They were okay."

"They were from store-bought dough. That's all Uncle Nate said he could make. And we still burned them."

Emery did her best to ignore the fluttering in her stomach at the image of the tough, virile man who could lift her heavy suitcase without a blink standing in the kitchen in an apron making cookies with his nieces.

"I'm so sorry, honey," she murmured. She wasn't the only one missing her mother or the life she used to have this Christmas, though what these two little girls were suffering seemed so much harder.

"Listen, I'm not the greatest baker, but I do have a few good cookie recipes. Maybe we could find a day before Christmas and the three of us could whip something up."

Tallie, on her sister's other side, looked ecstatic at the offer. "Really? You mean that?"

"As long as your uncle doesn't mind."

"He won't mind," Claire assured her as she wiped at her eyes. "He loves cookies. He just doesn't know how to make them."

"Can we still make a hat like yours if we're making cookies?" Tallie asked.

"I'm sure we can figure out a way to do both," she answered, and was greeted with delighted smiles.

So much for her claim that she wanted to avoid Christmas this year, she thought as they spurred their horses toward the house. Now she was committed to helping the girls make cookies and sew a few presents. The biggest surprise of all was that she actually looked forward to it.

Claire's tears dried by the time they reached the barn. As they dismounted and began removing the saddles from the horses, she and Tallie chattered about Christmas and the things they had asked for that year. Emery was carrying the saddle to the tackroom when she heard the outside door open.

"Where have you two been?"

She frowned at the anger in Nate's voice and quickly set the saddle on its form and returned to the stalls.

"We went for a ride," Claire answered.

"You went to the Daltons, didn't you?"

"I had to give Tanner his homework," Tallie said. "I told you."

"And I said we would drive over as soon as I finished with the attorney. You know the new rules. You know you're not supposed to take the horses on your own, no matter what your parents might have allowed. I have to know where you are."

"We weren't on our own," Tallie protested. "You said we couldn't go unless we were with an adult. We had Ms. Kendall with us."

He turned on her, his features thunderous.

"You had no right to just ride off with them. Do you have any idea how worried I've been? I was just about ready to start a search party."

"I left you a note," Claire said. "You were busy with the man and I didn't want to bother you."

"I didn't see any note."

"I put it on the hall table. That's where we always put stuff for Mom and Dad to see."

He raked a hand through his hair, his features still taut and angry, though Emery saw the echo of worry in his eyes. "I must have missed it."

"We gave all the homework to Tanner and now you don't even have to take us, since you don't like going to the Cold Creek," Tallie said, her voice cheerful.

"Tanner's stepmom was making cookies," Claire added, holding out the bag to him. "She sent a bunch for us."

"Did she?"

"Yep," Tallie said. "And then Claire was sad about the cookies since we didn't make the ones we usually do and Emery said she'll help us make Christmas cookies this year. Wasn't that nice?"

Nate shifted his dark-eyed gaze in her direction and he didn't look at all pleased by what she thought had been a rather kind offer.

"I'm sure it was." He put enough doubt in his voice that it sounded as if he believed exactly the opposite. "Listen, why don't you girls head up to the house where you can get warm and set the table for dinner? I'll finish up with your horses and be up in a minute."

They agreed readily enough and a moment later, she was alone with him in the barn.

"I'm sorry if I overstepped," Emery said. "It won't happen again."

"I shouldn't have gone off on you like that. I was just worried. A storm's coming and I was afraid they would be caught up in it." He paused, giving her a careful look. "They told you they could go, didn't they?"

She remembered Claire's claims that she had told her uncle they were going. "I might have been given that impression," she admitted slowly. "But I should have made sure."

He led Cielo into a stall and began brushing the horse with practiced motions that told her even if he hadn't lived here in some time, he was no stranger to horses or ranching.

"Their parents gave them a little more freedom to come and go as they please. They're used to riding all over the ranch and even to the neighboring ranches, something I'm not completely comfortable with. It's been one of many small adjustments over the past few months."

"How long have their parents been gone?"

"Since September."

She wanted to ask him what had happened to them, but he spoke before she could come up with a tactful way to broach the subject.

"Look, you're only here for a few days." His words were clipped, abrupt. "I would appreciate it if you would stay away from the girls."

She stared, the words of sympathy she had been gathering crumbling to ash in her mouth. "Excuse me?"

He shrugged. "Nothing personal. I'm sure you're a nice lady and all. But Tallie and Claire have suffered enough loss the past few months. We're all struggling to find our way here together. It's hard enough for them to have strangers coming and going in their lives. That's one reason I'm thinking about scaling down the guest ranch part of the operation here. I'm doing my best to keep them separate from the few guests we still have. Going for horseback rides with you, making cookies, sewing hats. It's all too much. They're going to think they have some kind of relationship with you. When you head back east to your life, the girls are going to feel abandoned by one more person in their lives."

"A rancher and an armchair psychiatrist. An interesting combination." She tried and failed to keep the bite from her voice.

She was beyond annoyed, suddenly. Had she ever asked for the girls' company? No. Her whole intent in coming to Hope Springs had been to spend the holidays alone, not to suddenly find herself responsible for the emotional well-being of two orphaned little girls. She was only trying to be kind to them, not trying to insinuate herself into their lives.

"I'm no psychiatrist, armchair or otherwise," he answered. "Or a rancher, for that matter. I'm only an army Ranger who's far more at home with my M4 carbine in my hands than a curry comb these days. I don't know a damn thing about raising two little girls. I'm going completely on instinct here—that's all I can do, really—and my gut is telling me it's not good for them to become too close to you."

Emery fought the urge to pick up the hayfork leaning against the stable wall and bash him over the head with it. Of course, if he was a highly trained soldier, he would probably have it out of her hands before she could even think about using it.

He was the girls' guardian, she reminded herself. It was

his right—and obligation—to act in whatever way he thought was in their best interest.

"I will certainly do my best to stay out of their way," she finally answered. "But I refuse to be cold or rude to them when our paths cross, just to pander to your paranoia. It's not in my nature."

"I can see that. I wouldn't want you to be rude," he answered and she could almost see his tongue dip into his cheek at the words.

She scowled. "The girls asked *me* to go riding and to help them sew hats for their friends. I did offer to help them make cookies, but only because Claire was distraught over missing that particular holiday tradition, not because I was trying to worm my way into their lives. I have work enough of my own to do. I thought I was coming to Idaho for seclusion and peace, not to entertain two lost, lonely little girls. Maybe before you start warning your guests to stay away from Claire and Tallie, you ought to ask yourself what they're missing from *you* that prompts them to latch onto the first kind stranger who comes along."

He drew in a breath, but she didn't give him an opportunity to respond to her counterattack; she just turned on her heels, thrust open the barn door and marched out into the fading December afternoon.

He deserved that, he supposed.

Nate watched his guest flounce out of the barn and winced as he remembered his accusatory tone. He had certainly botched yet another of his interactions with her. What was it about the woman that brought out the worst in him? He considered himself a pretty decent guy, for the most part. He usually tried to treat women with respect and appreciation. But without even trying, Emery Kendall seemed to hit all his hot buttons. She was sleek and cultured and sophisticated.

In comparison to all that blond perfection, he felt stupid and rough-edged. Just the poor dumb Mexican kid of the town whore.

He checked the horses one last time then left the barn. He really sucked at this whole hospitality thing. He wanted to shut the gates of Hope Springs and keep everybody out, guests and interfering neighbors alike.

He supposed that made him sound like some kind of hermit. He wasn't. He liked people, for the most part, and considered the others in his unit a genuine brotherhood.

But coming home to Pine Gulch seemed to bring out the worst in him. All the childhood pain and shame and confusion, those demons he had worked so hard to exorcise after he left came bubbling back up from somewhere deep inside, like one of those sulfur hot pots not far away in Yellowstone, oozing and ugly and acrid.

He looked over at Emery's cabin, where the lights glowed merrily against the gathering twilight.

She was only looking for a quiet place to spend the holidays, she had said. She was paying for a quiet escape. Whether he wanted to be running a guest ranch or not, he had opened the gates and allowed her in, so he was stuck—at least until he figured out what to do with Hope Springs and with the girls who had been left in his care.

Whatever she might be running from, whatever the cause of those secrets he could see in the deep blue of her eyes, he owed it to her not to let the hot mess of his life, both past and present, spill over and burn her.

* * *

Emery woke up to pitch darkness, bitter cold, and the vicious howling of wind beneath the eaves.

For a moment, she couldn't remember where she was, but as her eyes adjusted to the darkness, she registered the thick weight of the down comforter, the sturdy hollows and curves of the log ceiling above her, the flannel sheets that were worlds different from the 600-threadcount Egyptian cotton she used at home, but somehow comforting nonetheless.

Idaho. She was staying at a cabin in Cold Creek Canyon, just a short distance from the Daltons.

That deduction left her with two further mysteries for her sleep-numbed mind to work through. Why was she so blasted cold? And what had awakened her from fragmented dreams of her empty arms and her empty heart?

A loud banging rang out through the cabin from the other room, far too sharp and urgent to be something random from the wind she could hear howling under the eaves.

She really didn't want to leave protection of the blankets in order to check it out. If she was this cold with the covers tucked to her chin, how much worse would it be when she pushed them away?

"Ms. Kendall? Emery?" a man's low voice pushed through the howling wind and the stubborn cobwebs of sleep. Nate Cavazos, she realized.

"Coming," she called out, trying to gather her scrambled thoughts together. She reached for the bedside lamp, still not completely familiar with the cabin's layout to make her way in pitch darkness.

The light didn't switch on and she frowned. *That* must be why it was so dark and so cold in here. That storm howling out there must have cut the power, which meant the electric fireplace wasn't working, either.

Though everything inside her protested the invasion of even more cold, she managed to push away the covers and scramble in the blackness for the slippers she had left by the side of the bed. She might have to climb out of what little warmth she had left, but she wasn't about to touch her bare feet to the icy wood floor.

"Ms. Kendall?" Nate called again, raising his voice louder to be heard over the roar of the wind.

"I'm coming. Just a moment."

Groping her way in the dark, she made her way through the doorway of the bedroom then cursed when she cracked her knee on the mission rocking chair her outstretched hands must have missed.

She finally found the door, more by instinct than sight, and fumbled with the locks. She yanked it open then caught her breath as wind and snow swept inside in a mad icy rush.

Through the swirling snow, she could barely see Nate in the glow of the small lantern he held. He looked big and dark and dangerous. She remembered their tense discussion earlier in the barn and every instinct cried out for her to shove the door against him.

She ignored them all and opened the door farther. "It must be brutal out there. Come inside out of the wind." Her voice still sounded raspy and she tried to clear the sleep out of it as he pushed past her into the small cabin.

She was instantly aware of the heat emanating from him despite his snow-covered winter coat.

"Power's out. Guess you figured that out by now. I tried to start the generator for you behind the cabin, but the damn thing's being stubborn."

Ah. No wonder she was quickly turning to a solid block of ice.

"Does this happen often?" she asked, grateful she could see enough from his lantern light to grab the nubby throw off the back of the couch and wrap it around her.

He shrugged. "Sometimes. When I was a kid, I remember the power would go out just about every time we had a bad snowstorm. I think it's a combination of the wind and the heavy snowfall dragging down the power lines that run up the canyon. I don't expect it will be out for long. Maybe a few hours. Meantime, I'm afraid you'll have to come up to the house while we wait for the power crews to fix it."

She wrapped the throw more tightly around her. "Why? Don't you think I should be warm enough if I huddle under the blankets and put my coat on?"

"You have no idea how the windchill can work its way even through the best chinking in these log structures. I don't feel right about leaving you down here in the cold. We've got another generator at the house, plus a couple of wood fireplaces that can keep things plenty toasty. The girls are already camped out in the great room with their sleeping bags. We can find space for one more."

Near the girls he had warned her in no uncertain terms to stay away from? She might have a difficult time doing that when they were sharing the warmth of a fireplace. "Aren't you afraid I'll suck them further into my dastardly plan to break their little hearts when I leave Pine Gulch?"

He frowned and she felt bad for her sarcasm when she saw his mouth tighten with discomfort.

"This is an emergency and can't be helped," he answered. "These walls don't have much insulation. I can't leave you down here with no heat source. Even an hour in this cold could be deadly."

The gravity in his voice disconcerted her. She swallowed. As much as she wanted to lash back after his blistering words this afternoon, perhaps this wasn't the time. He *had* come down in the howling storm to make sure she was warm and safe. She ought to be grateful he didn't let her freeze to death.

"Can you give me a moment to change my clothes and put a coat on?"

"As long as it's only a moment. I don't like leaving the girls alone up at the house in this kind of weather. Here. Use the lantern. I've got a flashlight."

She nodded and reached outside the throw to take it from him. As she did, something hot flashed in his dark eyes for just an instant then was gone, and she realized that while her silk long underwear wasn't what anyone could call sexy, it still clung to every curve.

Her heart pounded at what she considered completely unreasonable speed. She snatched the lantern from him and hurried to the bedroom, closing the door firmly behind her. Inside, she quickly slipped a soft mint-green velour workout suit over her long underwear, then ran a brush through her sleep-tangled hair and pulled it back into a ponytail.

If she had any sense, she would pack up her rented SUV right this moment, head back to the airport and catch the first flight back to Virginia.

Whatever happened to her peaceful escape? She never expected Mother Nature to thrust her into this awkward situation, forced to spend even more time with a man who obviously wanted her out of his life.

Her sigh puffed out a little breath of condensation. She could handle this. With luck it would only be for an hour or two, then the power would be back on and she could hole up back here at the cabin until she finished the Spencer Hotels project, not venturing out until the holidays were over.

When she returned to the living room, she found Nate waiting for her just inside the door. Unfortunately, her boots were on the mat right beside where he was standing and there was no room around the furniture in the small space for her to grab them without being practically on top of him, an image she absolutely did *not* need racing through her head right now.

"I, um, need my boots," she said, gesturing to them.

"Oh. Right." He moved as far as he could in the other direction, but she still barely had space to squeeze past the table and grab them.

She was aware of the heat emanating from him. If there were more light in the small space, she wouldn't be surprised to see steam puffing off his coat. Was he always this warm or was it only the contrast between his body heat and the icy air inside her cabin?

She pushed away the question as completely irrelevant and focused on shoving her feet into her boots and throwing on her coat.

"Ready?" he asked, barely veiled impatience in his voice.

"As I'll ever be," she muttered.

He opened the door and the breath was snatched from her lungs by the cold and stinging snow.

"I'll take point on the way back to the house," he said, and she remembered him referring to himself as an army Ranger. She could easily see him parachuting out of an airplane over hostile territory or leading a team into a hostage situation somewhere.

"Just hold on to my coat and follow my tracks in the snow and you should be okay," he growled over the wind.

She might have thought the warning was overdramatic, maybe even intended to scare her, but the moment they stepped off the porch, the wind and snow raged even harder. She could see nothing but black with frenzied swirls of snow beyond the pale light from the lantern and the more focused beam of his flashlight.

As they began their painstaking trudge through the snow, she almost laughed when she remembered how she had thought the snow the night before was a blizzard. Compared to this, that was just a mild flurry. She could barely make out any kind of landmark in the darkness without any ambient glow from a porch light or a vapor light and what she could see was buried in snow.

She remembered reading in school once about how early pioneers were sometimes forced to run a rope between their house and barn during blizzards so they could hang on to it to safely while they made their way back and forth to take care of their livestock. Without that anchor, they could become hopelessly lost in moments and freeze to death before they found their way back home, not ever knowing they might be a few feet from their door.

She clutched the hem of Nate Cavazos's coat like it was her only lifeline, the only safe thing she had to hold on to in this surreal landscape.

At last, when her lungs were heaving from the cold and from the rapid pace the man set for them through knee-high snow, they reached the porch. He gripped her elbow to help her up the steps that hadn't yet seen a shovel and then he opened the door to the main ranch house.

Though she could still see the condensation of her breath here, blessed warmth from the fire crackling in the great room eased its steady way through the house and into her aching muscles.

Compared to the fury that lurked outside the door, it felt like the tropics in here.

She set the lantern down on the console in the hall and shook snow off her coat and took off her hat, this time a wool creation her assistant at the store knitted out of one of their custom yarns.

"Go ahead and hang your coat on one of the hooks," he said. She shrugged out of her coat and complied, aware as she did that he wasn't removing his own. Was he really going back out into that storm? she wondered. Before she could ask, though, two little dark heads peeked around the doorway.

"You're back!" Tallie exclaimed. She came into the entry with a brightly striped afghan wrapped around her shoulders. Beneath it, Emery saw she wore blue footie pajamas. Claire followed close behind with a matching afghan around her shoulders, but a plaid flannel nightgown several inches too short and fuzzy pink slippers peeking out below.

Tallie hugged her uncle, despite the clumps of snow clinging to his coat. "We thought maybe you were lost in the storm, Uncle Nate. You were gone *forever*."

The girl sniffled and Emery heard the deep fear in her voice. Her heart ached for this child who would probably never stop worrying she would lose someone else she loved.

For a moment, the man looked a little panicky at her

tears, but after an awkward moment, he pulled her into a hug and kissed the top of her glossy hair.

"Nope. I'm right here. I just had some trouble with the generator at the cabin so I had to bring Ms. Kendall back with me before she turned into a Popsicle. It sure is blowing out there. If not for the snow and the cold, it would be a good night for flying kites."

Both girls giggled, as Emery realized he had intended. Though she wasn't inclined to like him very much right now she had to approve. His teasing hit just the right note with his two frightened nieces.

"I'm so glad you're safe," Tallie said. "And you, too, Ms. Kendall."

To her shock, the girl left her uncle's side and slid her arms around Emery's waist. She smelled of shampoo and laundry detergent with an undertone of smoke from the fireplace and Emery felt a curious tug at her heart.

"Come in by the fireplace. It's *freezing* out here," Claire ordered.

She followed her into the great room and wanted to just stand and bask in the heat from the fire blazing merrily in the river rock hearth.

She was struck again by how bare the room was, with that empty Christmas tree and that massive rock mantel that cried out for some sort of natural garland of pine boughs.

The room was large, with two different furniture settings, two large sofas and an easy chair that made a U shape around the fireplace and a separate sitting arrangement in one corner near the Christmas tree. Both sofas were covered in blankets that had probably been dragged from other rooms in the house.

It was a comfortable room that could be genuinely

lovely with a few little touches. But that was none of her business, she thought.

"I need to go back out and check on the livestock and bring in some more logs," Nate said. "Will you all be okay in here?"

"Do you have to?" Tallie asked, a plaintive, worried note in her voice.

"Sorry, bug, but I do."

"Be careful," Claire said in the bossy tone Emery was beginning to realize was second-nature to the girl.

"I shouldn't be long," he said. "There should be plenty of wood to keep the fire going. Stay warm in here."

Though the girls looked worried after he left, they quickly shifted their attention to Emery.

"You can sleep on one of the couches," Claire said in a managing sort of voice that reinforced Emery's earlier impression that the girl was used to doing all she could to keep order in her world.

Still chilled from trekking through the snow, she sat as close as she could to the fire and wrapped a soft wool blanket around her shoulders. Tallie immediately sat beside her, only a few inches away, though the couch was broad and longer than normal.

"Will the horses be okay?" Tallie asked.

"I'm sure they'll all be fine. Horses are smart creatures and they'll head for any available shelter during the storm. Don't worry."

A particularly intense gust of wind rattled the huge picture window suddenly and the younger girl gasped and moved even closer.

"I really don't like the wind," she muttered.

"Don't be such a baby," Claire made a show of rolling

her eyes, but Emery was quite certain she saw apprehension in the other girl, as well, as she sat on her other side.

"I don't like the wind, either," Emery admitted.

"But you're a grown-up."

"Sometimes grown-ups are afraid of things too," she answered calmly. Heaven knows, she could bore them senseless with all the things that kept her up at night. "Shall I tell you a story my mother used to tell me when I was a little girl?"

"Please," Tallie begged, snuggling closer.

She settled deeper into the sofa. "The north wind and the sun one day had an argument about who was the stronger and could more easily remove a traveler's coat…"

She dragged the story out as long as she could, embellishing with several details that had never been in the original story. Then she added another and another and by the time her voice trailed off, both girls were half-asleep. Tallie stirred a little as Emery stopped speaking, but then eased back down again.

Emery closed her eyes as the fire crackled and hummed, its warmth both a physical and a mental comfort. This wasn't at all a bad way to spend a snowy night, she thought, just before she drifted off.

Chapter Four

When Nate returned to the house an hour later, exhausted and chilled to the marrow of his bones by the intense storm, he found the power still out, the fire burned down to embers and Emery and both girls sleeping on one couch.

He added another log to the fire and watched to make sure the embers would ignite it, then turned back to the sleeping females.

Emery dozed on one end, her cheek on the armrest, and both girls were cuddled together like puppies at the other.

The familiar, heavy weight of duty pressed down on his shoulders as he looked at his nieces. He loved them and had from the moment each was born, though he hadn't had much more than a distant, avuncular interest in them over the years.

That love had certainly grown in the past four months, but he had also discovered that instant fatherhood was far more terrifying than any challenge he had ever faced. Even being trapped in an Afghanistan mountain pass by a Taliban ambush and having to wait thirty-six hours for their exit transport had been easier than finding himself responsible for the emotional and physical well-being of Tallie and Claire.

It was enough to make even the most hardened of soldiers long to just pack up his gear and go AWOL.

He wouldn't. He owed his sister far too much for that, but sometimes he wondered how the hell he could survive the task ahead of him. Just thinking about them turning into teenagers and all that would come with that was enough to turn his hair gray.

Day by day, he reminded himself. That was the only way the three of them could make it through. One feeble, awkward step at a time. He just hoped to hell it would get easier.

He shifted his gaze to the other end of the couch toward his unwilling houseguest. In sleep, she was remarkably lovely, with those elegant debutante high cheekbones and that silky tangle of hair in a loose ponytail over her shoulder. His hands itched to pull it free, to bury his fingers in all that softness….

He had been far too long without a woman.

He sighed. That part of his life was in an indefinite holding pattern, much to his regret. How could he even think about women, about easing those particular appetites, when he had all these other damn plates spinning? The girls, the ranch, working out the details of Suz and John's estate?

If ever there was a woman who might make him change his mind about that, it was Emery Kendall, with that luscious mane of hair and her long, sleek legs and blue eyes that reminded him of a mountain lake on a clear, pure July afternoon.

As he watched, her long lashes fluttered and then opened. Disoriented confusion flickered in her gaze for an instant, followed quickly by alarm. He frowned. Why the hell would she be afraid of him, especially after he had risked frostbite to get her up here to the ranch house in safety?

He was only slightly appeased when she made an effort to steady her nerves. She sat up and wiped at her eyes.

"Sorry I woke you," he murmured. "I was just adding another log to the fire."

"No power yet, I guess," she whispered.

"Not yet. If lines are out around the valley, it might take the power company until morning to get out this way."

She nodded and extricated herself from the girls, who didn't even stir as Emery slid from the blankets, rearranged them, and stood silhouetted by the fire's glow.

His unruly body stirred. She definitely had curves in all the right places, something he *didn't* want to notice right now. He also didn't want to see how pretty and warm and slightly mussed she looked just waking up.

To his dismay, she walked nearer, probably so they could talk without disturbing the girls. Unfortunately, her proximity only intensified his awareness of the quiet intimacy here in the darkened house and the seductive scent of her, of vanilla and cinnamon and luscious, sleepy woman.

"How are the horses?" she whispered.

It took all his control not to step away from temptation. "Okay, as far as I can tell. Annabelle, one of our foaling mares, seemed a little restless but I'm sure she was just edgy about the storm. I'm afraid we're going to lose the roof on one of the hay sheds. It's metal and some of the sheets don't seem as secure as I'd like, but it's not safe in the dark and the wind for me to climb up and check."

"I should say not!" she exclaimed, slightly louder than a whisper. Claire stirred a little, but then seemed to settle back down.

He eased away from the fireplace toward the other end of the great room where they could speak slightly above a whisper. The fire's warmth reached here, though she still picked up a blanket and wrapped it around herself before she joined him.

"Were the girls all right?" he asked.

"Tallie doesn't like the wind. She was a little nervous at first, but Claire and I managed to settle her down. We told some stories and then they both fell asleep."

"I guess it was good you were here so I didn't have to leave them alone longer than necessary."

"They were worried about you."

"Yeah. They're both a little paranoid something's going to happen to me."

She was silent for a long moment and he braced himself, sensing the direction of her thoughts even before she spoke.

"What happened to their parents?" she finally asked.

He sighed, hit again by the grief for the sister he had loved. "Plane crash. John was a pilot with a share in a little Cessna in Idaho Falls. They left the girls with friends—the Daltons, actually—for a weekend so they could fly up to Glacier National Park for their anniversary. They had engine trouble on the way back and the plane lost altitude. John tried to make an emergency landing in a rainstorm, but he didn't have a clear spot and they ended up crashing into the mountains up near Helena."

He hated thinking of his sister's last moments, the terror she must have experienced as the plane went down. He was quite certain her last thoughts would have centered on what would happen to her girls. He only hoped she had somehow known he would step up, no matter how hard it might turn out to be.

He was also fully aware of the irony. He had been the special forces soldier, performing dangerous mission after dangerous mission, but it had been soft, homebody Suzi who had died so tragically and unexpectedly.

"Oh, those poor girls," Emery murmured. "No wonder Tallie is so nervous about bad weather. Where were you when it happened?"

"My third tour in the war against terror. Afghanistan, this time."

"So you came home?"

He hadn't seen any other choice. The girls had no one else. He could have sent them into foster care, but that would be a miserable way to repay the sister who had sacrificed so much to take care of him.

"I was close to the end of my commitment so I was able to work it out with the army to take the rest of the leave coming to me and get out early."

He hadn't wanted to. He had expected to make the army his career as long as they would still have him. But sometimes life threw a curveball and you either had to hit back or get cold-cocked in the face.

"May I ask you a question?" she asked after a moment.

"Shoot."

"I know it's presumptuous of me and you don't have to answer if you don't want to. It's really none of my business. But why isn't the Christmas tree decorated? Christmas is only a week away."

He glanced at the bare tree as guilt pinched him. Here was yet another way he had failed the girls. The three of them had brought the artificial tree down from the attic the week before and put it together, fully intending to decorate the blasted thing, but that was as far as they'd gotten.

Every day he told himself he would put the lights on it, but something always came up. A problem with one of the horses, a meeting at school, this blasted endless wrangling with the attorneys executing John and Suzi's estate.

Here was just another way he was failing the girls, though they hadn't once pushed him to finish decorating the tree all week. On some level, he suspected they were struggling just as he was to find a little holiday spirit somewhere.

"It's on the list. None of us has been much in the mood for Christmas," he admitted now to Emery.

"I hear you there," she murmured.

He wondered again at her history, why she was choosing to spend the holidays hiding away here at Hope Springs. He didn't need to know, he reminded himself. She was a guest, nothing more, and he would do well to keep that in the front of his head.

"We'll get to it, though," he said. "I was thinking maybe tomorrow or Sunday."

"Good. That's very good. They're children. I'm sure I don't need to tell you, but they need a Christmas tree. Stockings. Christmas cookies. All of it."

He had tried to make cookies, but the whole thing had ended in a disaster. Just like nearly everything else he tried.

"I have no idea how to throw Christmas for a couple of girls."

He hadn't meant to confess that and he was vaguely horrified that the words slipped out.

She gazed at him for a long moment and in the flickering light from the fire, her features looked fragile and as lovely as a painting.

"I could help you. At least with the decorating part."

He stared at her, stunned into speechlessness at the offer.

When his silence dragged on, she looked away and he saw annoyed frustration in her eyes. "Oh, right. I'm sorry, I forgot for a moment that you want me to stay away from the girls. I guess it slipped my mind while they were sleeping on the couch with me after you left them in my care."

His mouth tightened at her dry tone. Okay, he had been guilty of a bit of a double standard, grateful for her presence here with the girls during the storm when it was convenient for him, just hours after he told her he didn't want her spending more time with them.

He wanted to instinctively protest that he didn't want or need anyone's help, but that would have been a bald-faced lie. The second part, anyway. He might not want it, but he couldn't deny that he needed it, even to himself.

"What did you have in mind?" he asked warily.

"I could easily help the girls decorate the tree and put a little Christmas spirit into the house, at least," she said. "It's…sort of my specialty."

"Decorating Christmas trees?"

"Decorating in general. I'm a textile designer. Curtains, pillows, furniture upholstery, that sort of thing."

He blinked at that. Here was yet another example of just how far apart his world was from Ms. Emery Kendall's. The closest he came to designer textiles was buying a bed-in-a-bag set at the Wal-Mart near the base between deployments.

He could just imagine her reaction to the mess the ranch was in right now. Joanie had been doing basic housekeeping for him here between her minimal guest ranch duties, but since she left, he knew he had let plenty of things slide around the house.

"We're pretty simple and straightforward around here. We just need a Christmas tree decorated, not some fancy froufrou interior design," he said slowly.

She smiled a little and he immediately wished she hadn't. She looked far too warm and approachable when she smiled and he needed to remember all those differences between them. "I can do simple. Trust me, Nate."

He wanted to. The impulse to trust her, to lean on someone else for something, just for a little while, shocked the hell out of him. What was the big deal? She was offering to help put up some Christmas ornaments, not move in and start redecorating the whole place.

He worried the girls would latch onto her and be hurt when she left. But he supposed if he talked to them and made sure they understood that her presence in their lives was temporary, they could make it through.

"Fine. Whatever. Even if they haven't been in a hurry to put it up, Tallie and Claire will probably enjoy having a tree."

"You won't?"

He shrugged. "I don't do Christmas. Not really. It's been a long time since it meant something more than maybe a little extra chow in the mess hall to me."

"Do you miss it?" she asked quietly after a long moment. "The army, I mean."

He thought of the heat and the sand, the exhaustion and the constant, alert tension. He didn't think somebody who spent their time designing curtains would understand how he could miss it every single moment of every single day.

"This is my life now. The girls and the ranch."

She tilted her head to look at him and for a long moment, their gazes held. Something simmered between them, something bright, intense. Flames licked at the log in the fire, then consumed it in a shower of sparks.

He was powerfully drawn to her. If he moved just so, he could find out if that lush mouth was as sweet and delicious as it looked....

He leaned forward just a few inches, but the instant he realized what he was doing, he jerked back, furious at himself.

"You should sleep while you can."

Her blue eyes had darkened, he thought, until they were nearly the color of the Idaho midnight sky, but then she blinked and they seemed to go back to normal. "What about you?" she asked.

"I will. Eventually. I'd better go bring some more wood up to the house, just to be safe. If the power comes back on, I'll wake you so you can go back to your own cabin."

And out of my life, where you belong.

He didn't say the words, of course, though he wanted to. Still, he thought he saw something deep and bruised flare in her eyes as if she understood everything he had left unspoken.

"Good night, then."

She wrapped the quilt tighter around her shoulders and returned to the sofa by the fireplace.

He stood for a long moment in the doorway, watching her settle back in to sleep and fighting the impulse to go after her and apologize.

He finally slammed his hat onto his head and headed back into the storm. He had nothing to apologize for but his thoughts. He couldn't help it if he *did* think it would be better for all of them if she returned to her East Coast life and left him to deal with his two grieving nieces as he saw fit.

Still, she had been nice enough to offer her help with

decorating the house. He couldn't turn her down, especially since he knew the girls would probably enjoy helping her.

He fought his way through the blowing snow to the woodpile and loaded his arms with as much as he could carry then trudged back to the house. He could come up with no genuine reason to refuse her help, unfortunately. But that didn't mean he had to pretend to be happy about it.

Emery awoke to the smell of coffee and burnt toast and the sound of giggling girls and machinery rumbling somewhere outside.

She blinked a few times, struggling to find her bearings. The soaring log walls came into focus and the gray stones of the fireplace and then she spied two little dark-haired girls peeking around the doorway at her.

Ah. Right. She was at the main ranch house because a storm had wreaked havoc through Cold Creek Canyon.

Through her sleep-numbed brain, she managed to put together a few salient points. The power must have come back on, unless Nate had the small appliances in the kitchen wired to the generator he had mentioned the night before. Or, she supposed, unless he had made his toast and coffee over an open flame.

That growl of machinery must be Nate digging them out with the tractor she had seen him using to plow the snow the day after she'd arrived.

She sat up and scrubbed her hands over her face as relief soaked through her that she wouldn't have to face him yet this morning. She had stayed awake far too long, reliving that moment when heat and hunger had flared in his eyes, when she had been quite certain he wanted to kiss her.

Sometime later, she had heard him come in. When he

had walked into the room to check on the girls, she had fiercely feigned sleep, forcing her breathing to be slow and even, despite the pulse pounding loudly in her ears.

She drew in a breath now, remembering those long, drawn-out moments he had stood in the doorway before he turned and left the room. Either he had decided to stay up all night or he had found somewhere else moderately warm to sleep. He certainly hadn't used the other sofa. She would have known, since her own sleep had been light, unsettled.

"Oh, good! You're finally awake," Claire exclaimed now, hurrying into the room.

"What time is it?" Emery asked in a voice that only croaked a little.

"Almost seven," Tallie reported. "We've been up for *hours.*"

"Hours? Wow. I guess I must have been tired."

"Uncle Nate said we should let you sleep so we were trying to be super quiet. But we made toast. Do you want some?"

Few things smelled as sharply awful as burnt toast, but she smiled anyway. "Toast sounds great. I guess the storm stopped."

Tallie nodded. "It snowed a *lot.* Uncle Nate said he could barely open the back door for the drifts."

She could imagine. From her vantage point, all she could see out the wide pitched windows was a world of white.

"It's a good thing we rode over to the Cold Creek yesterday to take Tanner's homework," Claire said solemnly. "Uncle Nate says the horses could never make it today. He said we'll probably have to stay inside most of the day and with all the snow, it's going to be ice-cold out there."

"I don't like to be inside," Tallie complained. "It's so boring."

Without their parents, she imagined the house must seem to echo with silence. Poor little things.

She stood up and reached behind to readjust her ponytail, which she could only guess looked pretty bedraggled right about now. "Well, I can promise, you won't be bored today. You'll only *wish* you could find a quiet moment. Girls, we've got work to do."

They gave her matching looks of suspicion out of charmingly similar features. "What kind of work?" Claire asked.

Emery smiled at them both, marveling that the prospect of doing the very thing she had tried to avoid this year—wallowing in a little Christmas spirit—should lift her mood so effectively.

For a fleeting moment, she thought of her mother and how she had so enjoyed Christmas. Their house in Warrenton had always exploded with lights and ornaments and holiday cheer. She wouldn't have wanted Emery to firmly close the door on the holidays this year out of her grief and sorrow. Her mother would have been the first one to help these lonely little girls.

"You'll see," Emery said. "I think you're going to need a little more than toast for breakfast. What do you say to pancakes?"

"I say de-lish," Tallie said with that adorable grin of hers.

"Yum," Claire said. "I've been thinking I should learn how to make pancakes. Uncle Nate tries, but his are all squishy and gross."

She smiled. "Give me a few minutes to freshen up a bit and then we'll eat. And then, my dears, we go to work."

Chapter Five

Thirty minutes later, she was frying a package of lean bacon she'd found in the refrigerator and overseeing Claire at the griddle while Tallie colored at the kitchen island.

"Now see, when the batter starts to bubble on the top, that's when you know they're ready to be turned."

"That must be where Uncle Nate goes wrong," Claire said, her brow furrowed. "I wonder if he knows the batter is supposed to bubble."

"I'll be sure to mention it to him if I get the chance," Emery said, unable to completely hide her smile.

"Here he comes," Tallie proclaimed. "You can tell him now."

Sure enough, a moment later, she heard boots thudding on the back steps and a moment later, the mudroom door off the kitchen opened.

Her stupid, reckless heart caught in her chest as she remembered those intense few moments the night before, the flare of heat in his dark eyes when she had been quite certain he wanted to kiss her.

"Hey, Uncle Nate!" Tallie called. "Emery knows why your pancakes never taste very good."

She flushed as he walked into the kitchen, stomping snow off his boots.

"Does she?" he asked slowly.

"She says the pancakes have to bubble first before you flip them. I think these are just about ready," Claire said, then she tucked her bottom lip between her teeth and shoved the spatula under one of the pancakes with all the solemn intensity of someone trying to extract explosives from a landmine.

"Remember, flipping is all in the wrist," Emery said.

Claire nodded and turned the entire batch just right, except for one that landed half on another.

"I messed up," she said with a disappointed frown.

"Just one," Emery said with a warm smile. "That's no big deal. Nobody can turn every pancake perfectly. You did great. They're going to taste delicious."

"Did you see that, Uncle Nate?" Claire exclaimed.

"I sure did." He hung his coat on the hook by the door. "I hope you've got a couple to spare for me. Running that tractor works up a real appetite."

"You can have as many as you want," Claire promised him. A moment later, she flipped a tall stack onto a plate for him and handed it over to her uncle.

"Wow. Delicious. I only came in to fill up my coffee, but this all just smells as good as it looks."

"Would you like some bacon?" Emery asked. His dark gaze slid to hers and suddenly all the heat that had seethed between them in the quiet stillness of the night burned through her once more.

"Bacon would be good, if you've got some to spare."

Doing her best to ignore her ridiculous reaction to him, she put several strips on a plate for him and set it at his elbow as he pulled up a chair beside Tallie at the table.

For the next few moments, she listened to their interaction. He complimented Claire on the pancakes so effusively that the girl had a warm, rosy glow of pride. Between mouthfuls of pancakes and bacon, he also admired Tallie's drawings, making a special point of telling her specifics he liked about her picture, like the way the pine branches of the Christmas tree she drew looked all feathery and real.

He loved them. It was obvious in every word he said to them. How difficult this all must be for him. She had heard that note of longing in his voice when she asked him the night before if he missed the life he had given up for them.

Though they would probably always grieve for their parents, the girls were extraordinarily fortunate that Nate would give up his career, his life, to return to Pine Gulch and raise them.

She didn't want to feel this softening toward him, this flutter of tender feelings, so she forced her voice to be brisk. "How much snow did the storm leave?" she asked.

He cast a quick glance at her then turned his attention back to his plate. "Hard to say, exactly, because of the wind. I'm guessing maybe eighteen inches, but we've got drifts four feet high in places. It's going to take most of the day to clear them out. Hope you weren't in a hurry to head down the canyon. I doubt the county will be getting to Cold Creek Canyon Road until tonight at the earliest."

She was trapped here with them. Or at least at the ranch.

Since the power was back on, she could return to her cabin and spend the day in isolation, trying to finish her sketches for the Spencer Hotels project.

"We're not going anywhere anyway," she answered. "Not for a while, at least. The girls and I have plans."

"Except you haven't told us what they are yet," Tallie complained.

"I'm sure you'll find out soon enough," Nate said with a sidelong smile to Emery that made her ridiculous heart kick up a notch.

"I hope it's something fun," Tallie said, trying to wheedle a little more information out of them.

"As soon as you're finished eating, why don't you to go change out of your pajamas into some clothes you can work in," Emery suggested.

"I'm done," Tallie jumped up and headed for the door.

"Me, too." Her sister quickly joined her and Emery could hear them racing each other up the stairway.

Too late, she realized her suggestion for them to change would leave her alone with Nate.

After a few more moments of eating in an uncomfortable silence, he pushed his plate away, finished off his coffee, then rose.

"I don't know how long I'll be out there. After I get us cleared out, I've got to see what I can do about fixing the hay shed. The wind took out a big section of the roof."

"Can you repair it by yourself?"

"I'll have to figure something out until I can get somebody out here to do the job right." He cleared his throat. "I hope it's okay if I leave the girls with you. I usually don't like to be gone from the house too long, but I don't have much choice. It's too cold for them out there."

"We've got plenty to keep us busy," she assured him. "Don't worry. We'll be fine."

He met her gaze again and she could swear she felt her heart knock against the walls of her chest. Ridiculous. She really had to reel in this insane reaction to him.

"Thanks. For breakfast and for…everything."

"You're welcome." She forced a smile, hoping it looked more genuine than it felt.

He studied her for a moment then slid away from the chair, reaching for his cowboy hat just as the girls hurried back.

"That was the quickest change on record," he said with a mock look of astonishment. "You two are like a couple of firefighters heading out on a call."

Claire rolled her eyes at him, but Tallie giggled.

"Are you going back in the cold?" the younger girl asked.

"Yeah. I've still got a lot of digging ahead of me. You girls do what Ms. Kendall says, okay?"

They gave him hugs as he bundled up.

"Be careful on the tractor," Tallie told him, her voice solemn. "Drew Wheeler's dad died in a tractor wreck."

"I'll be careful, I promise." He kissed her nose, wrapped his scarf around his neck and headed out into the cold again.

The kitchen was curiously empty without his presence. Both girls looked a little forlorn, but Emery summoned another smile.

"Let's clean up these dishes, then get to work."

"Your pancake recipe is very good," Claire said, her voice solemn. "Thank you for showing me how to make them. From now on, I won't forget about the air bubbles."

This serious child needed to laugh a little more often, Emery thought. The truly tragic thing was, she saw entirely too much of herself in Claire, a child so eager to please the remaining grown-ups in her life that she became an adult far too early.

Emery made a vow that she would do her best to see the girl enjoyed herself while they decorated the Christmas tree.

"Now will you tell us what we're going to do?" Tallie begged.

She hugged the girl's shoulders. "Get ready. The three of us are going to make some magic."

The storm kept Nate away from the ranch house most of the day.

After all the ranch access routes were plowed out and he had spent a couple hours doing a credible, if somewhat makeshift, job covering the exposed hay until the weather wasn't so cold and he could repair the roof properly, he headed down the canyon with the tractor to see if any of their neighbors needed digging out.

On the way, he passed Seth Dalton out on a tractor, as well, working on the driveway of Guillermo and Viviana Cruz, the Daltons' nearest neighbors. He lifted a hand in greeting to the man before he continued on his way.

He really wanted to despise all the Dalton boys, on principle if nothing else. He had certainly hated their father. Half of Pine Gulch did, though few of them had as personal a reason as Nate.

As far as Nate was concerned, Hank Dalton had been a genuine son of a bitch. He had lied and stolen and basically manipulated his way into owning half of Cold Creek Canyon. He had respected no boundaries.

Nate's hands tightened on the tractor controls. He hated Hank Dalton, even two decades after his death, but he couldn't quite bring himself to feed that hate by turning it against the man's sons.

They were difficult men to dislike.

Wade Dalton, who had taken over running the ranch after his father's death, seemed a fair man in his few dealings with him. Nate had seen him around town with his wife and a passel of children and it was obvious he doted on his family.

Jake, the middle brother, was the family physician in town. Nate had taken both girls to him in a panic a few months back when they'd both caught some bug and run fevers of a hundred and one. Doc Dalton had been patient and calm with the girls and had even taken time to allay Nate's brand-new-parent phobias about germs.

Seth, the youngest, had been Nate's own age and while they hadn't exactly been friends, they hadn't been enemies, either. Seth had seemed most like his father, at least where women were concerned. He used to run through them like irrigation water through sprinkler pipe, even in high school.

Nate had been shocked to come back to Pine Gulch and find Seth married to, of all people, the very respectable elementary school principal, a woman he liked and admired. By all appearances and the rumors he'd heard, theirs was an extraordinarily happy marriage and Seth's wild reputation seemed firmly in the past.

He supposed he and the Daltons could never be best friends. The vein of bitterness against their father ran too deep inside him for that and he couldn't seem to get past it. But they were neighbors for the time being, until he figured out whether he was going to sell the ranch, so he did his best to be polite.

He frowned as he reached the next ranchette down from

Rancho de la Luna as another little detail on his to-do list nipped at him. The girls were begging him to take them to a neighborhood party Caroline and Wade Dalton were throwing along with Carson and Jenna McRaven.

He had been putting them off and hadn't let the McRavens or the Daltons know whether he was going to show up. He was going to have to make a decision on that. But not right now, he thought as he lowered the snowplow. The party wasn't until Wednesday. That gave him three more days to make up his mind.

By late afternoon, he was cold and hungry and knew he had taken extreme advantage of Emery Kendall's presence at home with the girls. He had to get back and figure out what to fix them for supper, his least favorite part of instant parenthood.

He drove back to the ranch, hurried through the afternoon chores, then headed up to the house, bracing himself to face her wrath.

He entered by the front door, since it was closer to the barn, and walked into a winter freaking wonderland.

He stared around the house, delicious scents eddying around him. Onions and garlic and tomatoes, along with the underlying sweetness of something tasty baking.

Garlands of pine boughs and red and gold ribbons draped the log staircase and just about every doorway in sight. A vast collections of wood-carved Santas he vaguely remembered from one of the few visits he made back to the ranch during the holidays took up an entire corner display cupboard and a trio of thin evergreens stood in what had been an empty corner, draped in twinkling white lights and more of those red and gold ribbons.

He walked into the great room. This morning the tree

had stood barren and forlorn in the window, but now it was ablaze with lights and ornaments and more of those red and gold ribbons. It was topped by a huge gleaming tinsel star, one of the few Christmas traditions he remembered from his own childhood. What should have looked tawdry and outdated amid all the other decorations somehow looked wondrous and bright in the gathering dusk.

Had Suzi really tucked away all these ornaments somewhere or had Emery and the girls made some of them this afternoon?

He looked around, marveling at the difference a few little touches could make. This morning when he left to plow the snow, he thought it had been a nice, comfortable house. A little cluttered and dusty, maybe, since Joanie took off, but not a bad place. Certainly nicer than it had been when they were kids, for all the work Suzi and John had poured into it.

In the space of a few short hours, apparently Emery Kendall had gone to town and turned something average into something extraordinary.

She and the girls must have scoured every inch of the house and the attic to find all the decorations. A couple of quilts in Christmas colors had been hung on the walls alongside the one that traditionally hung there. The mantel was covered in a wild cluster of red, gold and white candles in a variety of thicknesses and heights.

The place looked warm and inviting. Happy, even.

He should have done this for them. This was a connection to their past and he couldn't let them lose it.

He drew in a breath, took one last look around at the wonder Emery and the girls had created, then turned to follow the delectable scents to the kitchen. They didn't hear him come in, probably because Christmas carols were blaring from the small under-cabinet stereo in the kitchen and Emery and the girls were all singing along.

The kitchen was a mess. Flour covered the surface of the island and at least three or four dozen sugar cookies cooled on racks on every inch of the countertops.

"Oh, look, here's a shape we haven't used yet," Emery said as she sorted through one of the bottom drawers he wondered if he had ever even looked inside. "It's a really cute angel. Look at those darling wings."

"Ooh, I want to cut out that one," Claire exclaimed, looking more animated than Nate had seen her since he came back.

"I'm going to put yellow wings on it and maybe a halo," Claire added.

"I don't want to use that one," Tallie said with that stubborn look she sometimes wore.

"Why not?" Emery asked, surprise in her eyes at Tallie's tone.

"Because it's fake. There are no such thing as angels."

The cynicism, so unusual in the typically bright and open Tallie shocked him. Nate frowned, lurking there on the other side of the door, just out of view.

"Why do you say that?" Emery sounded as surprised as he felt.

"My mom used to tell me we all had a guardian angel to watch over us," Tallie answered. "But I don't think that can be true at all. If it was, why didn't Mommy and Daddy's guardian angels hold up their airplane so they wouldn't crash?"

He drew in a sharp breath, quite certain Emery must be able to hear the sound of his heart shattering into pieces.

Every once in a while, the girls' raw grief reached out and socked him in the gut. He wished with everything inside him that he could ease this pain for them, make their world right again.

Maybe if he was a better substitute parent to them, they wouldn't have to stay up late at night thinking about these sorts of things, like guardian angels who had apparently fallen down on the job.

"Oh, honey." Emery's voice was soft and sad. "Sometimes even the very best of guardian angels can't stop bad things from happening. That doesn't mean you don't have angels watching out for you. The other night when I was driving here in a storm, I was sure my mom was with me making sure I made it here safely."

"Maybe she wanted you to get here so you could help us put up the Christmas tree," Claire said.

Emery laughed, though Nate was quite sure it sounded a little trembly. "You're probably exactly right."

"So why didn't the angels help my mom and dad?" Tallie asked plaintively. "Didn't they know me and Claire needed them?"

"I don't know the answer to that, sweetheart," Emery said after a long pause. "There are a lot of things I wish I knew the answer to. I can only tell you that I'm positive your parents would have wanted to stay with you more than anything. But I bet they're so happy you have an uncle who loves you deeply."

He must have moved or made some kind of sound, because Emery's head whipped around and their gazes met. So much for stealth, he thought as she gave him a charged look. He could tell she was wondering how much of the conversation he had overheard.

More than he wanted to, he thought, wishing again that he could make everything okay for the girls.

"Hi, Uncle Nate!" Apparently the moment of cynicism and disbelief had passed as Tallie greeted him with one of those rapidfire mood shifts that always disconcerted him and left him wondering if it was more a function of her age or her sex, as chauvinistic as he knew that made him.

"Hi." He returned her hug, still somewhat stiff and awkward at these spontaneous displays of affection, though he wanted to think he was improving. "So where are you hiding all the elves?"

"What elves?" Tallie asked.

"The ones who have been going crazy decorating the tree and hanging garlands everywhere and even making cookies."

Tallie giggled and even bossy, serious Claire broke a grin.

"No elves, Uncle Nate," Tallie assured him. "It was only us. Ms. Kendall and Claire and me. We did all the work. Every bit of it."

"Wow. I couldn't believe it when I walked it. I was sure I had come to the wrong place and walked into that Christmas store in Jackson Hole by mistake."

"You can have a cookie," Claire told him in that managing tone of hers that sometimes bugged the heck out of him, but just now seemed sweetly concerned for his well-being.

"Thanks. Don't mind if I do. Which one should I try?"

"A snowman," Tallie said. "I decorated that one with the red hat, see?"

He took a bite of the sugar cookie. It was soft and chewy and perfect. "Wow, that tastes terrific."

"I mixed the dough my very self," Tallie announced, looking pleased. "Claire only helped a little."

Her sister snorted. "Only because I was busy helping Miss Kendall make the rolls!"

Almost effortlessly, Emery stepped in to avert one of their potential bickerfests that could turn fierce in an instant. "I don't know what I would have done without help from each of you today. They knew where all the decorations were stored and helped me scour through every box."

"You all did a great job. The house looks…perfect."

Emery smiled at him and for an instant, the kitchen seemed to fade away and they were once more in the hush of the darkened house, talking quietly in the night while the girls slept. Just as the evening before, he wanted to kiss her with a ferocity that astonished him.

What the hell was the matter with him? She wasn't at all his type, he reminded himself. Beyond that, she was a guest at the ranch and beyond *that,* they were standing in a flour-covered kitchen with his two nieces looking on, for crying out loud.

"Would you like some soup?" Emery asked. "It's beef barley. I hope you don't mind, I helped myself to the ingredients in the pantry and found plenty of packaged meat in the deep freeze. I thought you might like something warm when you came in from outside."

"That would be great. It's been a long day."

"I'll get it for you, Uncle Nate," Claire said. He thought about telling her he was perfectly capable of dishing his own bowl of soup and she didn't have to wait on him, but she looked so eager to please he didn't have the heart.

"I'll get you one of the rolls," Tallie said. "They're really good, too. I had three of them."

"Thanks. I'll start with two."

For the next few moments, the girls fussed over him,

pouring him water, fetching utensils, grabbing a napkin, while Emery looked on with amusement.

He had to admit, it was kind of nice, though not a particular pleasure he was very accustomed to. It had been a long time since he'd been mothered. Longer still since it had been his own mother filling the role.

Emery had done all this, given the girls something to focus on besides their loneliness. He was grateful for her, but that didn't help the nagging worry.

They already were crazy about her. He could tell by the way Claire sought her opinion about decorating a cookie and how Tallie looked to her for approval as she rolled out more of the dough.

Hell, he could be halfway there himself if he spent any more time sharing quiet confidences in the dark.

He would just have to make sure that didn't happen, he told himself. And though the soup tasted delicious, he had a tough time eating more than a few spoonfuls past the sudden apprehension tightening his throat.

Chapter Six

Her soup must be truly terrible, if a man who had been working out on the ranch all day in the cold could barely stomach it.

Maybe she needed to double-check the seasonings. A bit too much pepper, perhaps? She couldn't quite believe that, especially since she had tried it earlier with the girls. They had eaten every bite and she had found it delicious, savory and rich and warming.

Nate, though, was glowering at it like it was flavored with alum and vinegar.

She had spent all day trying to make the ranch house more comfortable for him and for the girls. A little thanks might be nice, instead of this scowling, surly stranger who would barely look at her.

Maybe it wasn't the house or the soup he didn't like. More likely, it was her. He had made that plain enough the past few days, though she had hoped things might be different between them after the night before.

She wouldn't allow herself to be hurt. He *was* a stranger, one whose opinion shouldn't matter to her.

With a forced smile to the girls, she reached to untie the holiday-themed apron she had borrowed from the hook inside the pantry, the one Tallie had softly told her had been Suzi Palmer's favorite.

"That's the last batch of cookies. I think you can decorate the rest of them on your own, girls. I really need to head back to my cabin."

"No!" Tallie exclaimed. "You don't have to go yet."

"You should sleep here again," Claire said, worry clouding her eyes. "What if the power goes out again?"

Emery smiled, even as her heart clutched that this girl felt she had to shoulder responsibility for everyone in her world.

"No worries," she answered, hugging Claire's thin shoulders. "If the power goes out, I'm quite sure your uncle won't mind at all if I come back to the house, will you?"

Something flared in his eyes at the challenging note to her voice, but he didn't rise to the taunt. "Of course not," he said, his voice cool. "The storm has passed and has headed across Wyoming by now, but you can stay here tonight if you're worried."

She shook her head. "I'll be fine. I will take a little soup home with me if you don't mind, to warm up in the microwave for lunch tomorrow."

It took a few more moments than she would have liked to dish some of the soup into a container she had spied earlier in the cupboard, when she had been looking for measuring cups for the cookie dough.

While she thrust her feet into her boots and put on her

coat and scarf, Tallie and Claire continued to plead with her to stay one more night—and she continued to gently insist she needed to return.

Finally, Nate set the spoon back in the half-eaten soup bowl and scraped his chair back. "Girls, that's enough. Emery is staying at the ranch as our guest, not as your new favorite plaything. I'll walk you back," he said to her.

She gave him her best snotty debutante look, the one she and her girlfriends had perfected at their private girls' school for moments just like this, when they were faced with a stubborn, interfering male.

"That's completely unnecessary. I believe I know the way by now. Go ahead and finish your soup."

Nate didn't seem swayed by either the look or by her cool tone as he put his still-damp coat back on. "I need to make sure the power's working at the cabin anyway before I feel right about you staying there for the night. You girls finish up the cookies, then when I come back you can give me the grand tour of everything you did today, okay?"

"I'll keep an eye on things," Claire said, sounding about thirty years old instead of only eleven.

"Thanks," he answered, then thrust open the door for Emery. "You ready?"

Not wanting to argue with him in front of the girls, she only nodded stiffly and followed him outside.

She hadn't been outside since the middle of the night, that arduous trip through the blowing snow to the house. The wind had stopped, she was relieved to discover, but the cold still snatched away her breath. After only a few breaths, she was quite sure her lungs would freeze into icicles.

She was grateful to reach the cabin, even if it did look dark and cheerless compared to the festive ranch house they had left behind. He opened the door for her, flipped on the light inside, then, to her dismay, he followed her into the cabin.

"I'll just check the heat," he said.

"I can think I can flip the switch to turn it on all by myself. I'm not one of the girls. I've been taking care of myself for a long time."

He tilted his head as he studied her while the fan on the electric fireplace whirred to life, pouring blessedly warm air into the room.

"Why is that?"

"What?" she asked, confused.

"Why have you been taking care of yourself for so long? I'm sure this sounds chauvinistic, but I'm just wondering why there's no man in your life."

"How do you know there's not?" she snapped, not quite sure why she was so angry, but grimly aware she was more furious than she'd been in a long time.

He shrugged. "I might just be a dumb soldier from Idaho, but I can put a few minor details together and get the big picture. What kind of man lets his woman come out to the middle of nowhere to spend Christmas by herself? That tells me you've probably had a bad breakup in the not so distant past."

"You're not as smart as you think you are, Mr. Cavazos."

"I don't think I'm smart at all," he muttered. She thought she heard him add something else under his breath like "at least I haven't been since you showed up", but she didn't hear the words clearly and she wasn't about to ask him to repeat them.

"You're wrong about a recent bad breakup. My divorce was final eighteen months ago and the marriage was over six months before that. And there's been no one else."

She thought of that terrible Christmas two years earlier, when her perfect little world—everything rosy and bright she thought she had attained—came crashing down at her feet with only a few words and a careless moment behind the wheel.

Nate leaned his hip against the edge of the table, crossed his arms across his chest and studied her carefully with a baffled look in his eyes.

"What kind of damn fool walks away from a woman as beautiful as you, who can make beef barley soup that tastes like heaven?"

She stared at him, heat soaking through her at his words. She didn't want to think about the first part so she focused on the second. "I thought you hated the soup. You barely tasted it."

He raised an eyebrow. "Are you kidding? I wanted to stick my face in the bowl and just inhale the whole thing, but I figured that would probably be bad manners in front of the girls. After they're in bed, though, I might just have to dish up another bowl."

Nate Cavazos was a complicated man, she decided. Not as easily pegged as Jason or any of the other men she had known.

"That's beside the point. The question is, why the divorce?"

None of your damn business, she wanted to say. It was nothing less than the truth and was exactly what she should have said and what she intended to say when she opened her mouth. But somehow completely different words came out.

"Turns out, if a man cheats on you when you're college sweethearts, he's probably not going to change after you're married."

It had only been that one time, Jason had claimed. He had been drinking, she had been a sorority girl who came onto him. That had been the only time she had *known* about in college. She had stupidly taken him at his word when he said it was a one-time fling and meant nothing. If she had listened to her gut, she could have avoided so much pain later.

"He *must* be an idiot, then," Nate said now. "But at least you didn't have to drag any children through the mess of a divorce."

Her throat closed and she fought the instinct to cover her abdomen. Nate didn't need to know *everything*.

"Lucky, wasn't it?" she said, then cleared her throat, hoping he didn't hear the slightly ragged note in her voice. "Anyway, that's all in the past. I've *completely* moved on. Jason had nothing to do with my decision to come to Hope Springs for the holidays."

"Then why are you here?"

None of your damn business, she almost said again, but refrained. "Work. My mother died in September. She was…the only family I had left and I didn't want to face the holidays without her in the midst of all my friends and familiar surroundings. I needed a change."

"I guess you found that. Idaho blizzards are certainly out of the norm."

"True enough. I didn't expect quite the adventure I've discovered so far, but it hasn't been all bad."

"Well, thanks again for everything you did today. I should have decorated the tree weeks ago, not left it this late."

"The girls and I enjoyed ourselves."

"I could tell. A little too much, maybe." He made a rueful face. "I'm going to be taking down decorations until Valentine's Day."

"Take everything down now, if you hate it so much," she retorted sharply.

He looked baffled by her sudden attack, as well he should be, she thought. It had been unprovoked and unnecessary. *Just say good-night and push him out the door,* she thought.

"Did I say I hated any of it?"

"Not in so many words, maybe. But it's obvious you're not happy with how the girls and I spent our day."

He looked at her as if she were crazy. She *felt* a little crazy, and tired and out of sorts. She should have just kept her big mouth shut.

"Why do you think I don't like the decorations? I said thank-you, didn't I? I'm pretty sure I did."

Just go, she thought. "You did. I'm sorry. I'm just tired and cranky. It's been a long day following an…unsettled night."

There it was. The reason she was upset. She hadn't slept much, too stirred up by that moment when he had nearly kissed her—when she had desperately wanted him to, something she hadn't admitted until right this moment.

Suddenly the tension in the cabin ratcheted up a notch and when she finally looked up, she was afraid he could read her thoughts. He was staring at her mouth, his eyes intense, half-closed in a sexy sort of way.

"Well, good night," she finally said, about five blasted minutes too late, but even to her own ears, her voice sounded thready, smoky, even, and an instant later—before she could even think to take a breath—he stepped forward in one smooth, determined motion and captured her mouth.

She froze in shock. He smelled of the cold, like pine trees drooping with snow, but the heat of his mouth on hers made an arousing contrast. He tasted of coffee and her soup and the sweet aftertaste of the girls' sugar cookies.

And something else, something male and sexy and indefinably Nate.

She didn't intend to kiss him back. She slid her hands to his chest, fully intending to push him away. Instead, she suddenly found her fingers curled into the soft weave of his shirt beneath his unzipped coat. She could feel the enticing heat of him and she wanted to sink into it, into him.

With a soft little sound, she opened her mouth to his, all the curiosity and disappointment of the night before forgotten in a moment as that heat curled through her and wrapped around them both.

She didn't know how long they stood inside her cabin, their mouths tangled and the world outside her door forgotten. She only knew it had been entirely too long since she had felt this clutch of desire, this churn of her blood, the heat and wonder from a kiss that completely stole her breath and her reason in one fell swoop.

He was the one to break the connection. One moment he was there, hard and muscled and male, then next he was taking a step away from her and cold rushed in to take the place of all that heat.

They gazed at each other for a long moment, the only sound in the cabin their ragged breathing and the whir of the electric fireplace.

Finally he shook his head just a little, as if he couldn't quite believe what had just happened.

"Don't say anything," she said, her voice low as her cheeks flamed with embarrassment and lingering desire. She had never responded to a man with such instantaneous heat. "That should never have happened."

"No?"

"No! We're… You don't even like me."

"I wouldn't say that, exactly," he drawled.

What *would* he say, exactly? She didn't want to know, she told herself. "It was a mistake. We're both tired and the day has been…eventful. Let's both just pretend it didn't happen and move on."

"Right." His tone was skeptical, but he reached for the doorknob.

Emery thought of her mother, always scrupulously polite and well-mannered, the perfect hostess and law firm partner's wife. She tried to adopt the tone Catherine had perfected. "Thank you for walking me back. Good night."

He still looked somewhat dazed and she was almost certain his gaze dipped to her mouth again, but he only turned the knob.

"You can pretend all you want, I suppose," he finally said. "Good luck with that. But I have to tell you, I'm a pretty basic kind of guy. I'm afraid my powers of imagination won't stretch quite that far. I don't think I'll be forgetting it anytime soon."

He left before she could offer any sort of reply to that and she closed the door after him, wondering how one man could be so full of complications.

She pressed two trembling fingers to her mouth, to the heat and taste of him that still lingered there.

Good heavens, the man could kiss. For a brash, abrupt soldier, he had seduced her lips with consummate skill.

She hadn't been this attracted to a man in…well, ever. Yes, it had been a while since she had been involved with a man. She hadn't dated since her divorce, too busy first grieving the loss of the cloud castles she had created for her life and then coping with her mother's cancer diagnosis and her fight against the disease that eventually claimed her.

Perhaps that was the reason she wanted to melt in Nate Cavazos's arms like an ice cube tossed onto a sizzling hot engine.

She let out a breath. She wanted to believe her past two years of abstinence were responsible for her reaction to him, but she couldn't quite make herself buy that explanation.

Nate was the most powerfully physical man she had ever known. Men in her world wore designer suits and comfortably talked about the difference between twill and chambray.

Nate was all soldier, rough and dangerous and irresistible.

Some instinctively feminine part of her responded to all that energy, all that heat, and she just wanted to soak it all in. She sighed. It didn't matter the explanation for the unwilling attraction. She simply had to ignore it. In a week, she would be back in her real life and this would all be just a memory.

Mistake or not, she knew their kiss would linger in her mind for a long, long time.

Chapter Seven

He couldn't stop thinking about Emery Kendall and that kiss that had curled his toes.

Twenty-four hours later, Nate stood by the Christmas tree she had decorated in front of the big window, looking at the lights of her little cabin twinkle in the darkness.

Every once in a while, a shape moved past the curtain and he caught his breath, feeling like some kind of a damned voyeur.

That kiss. It had haunted his dreams through the cold night and then seemed to follow him around all day as he had hurried the girls off to school, spent the day at chores and doing a proper job on the hay shed roof, and then hurried into town after school for the parent-teacher conferences he would have blown off if not for a fortuitous call from the school secretary.

He couldn't forget the taste of Emery's mouth, lush and

inviting and far more sensually responsive than he might have expected from her.

His insides still clutched with hunger when he remembered that moment when she had curled her hands into his shirt and pulled him closer.

He shook his head at his own ridiculous reaction. He was in serious danger of making a fool out of himself over her. Polished society-type women didn't have the time of day for rough soldiers with the sand of the Middle East still stuck under their fingernails and an entire footlocker overflowing with problems and responsibilities.

He gazed at the reflection of the Christmas tree she had decorated flickering in the window.

He wasn't sure how she had done it, but in a few hours the day before, she had changed the whole mood of the house, brightened it somehow.

She hadn't made any huge changes. No long-forgotten antiques had been dragged out of the attics or anything. But a few little touches lent a warmth and homeyness to the place and seemed to push back the darkness a little.

He hoped the girls sensed it. He wanted to think they had been a little happier, especially Claire. Maybe it was the impending holiday or thinking about Christmas vacation that started in a few days, but he thought she had lost some of that pinched, uptight look around her mouth. After school when he was meeting with her teacher, she had smiled a little more than he was used to and had even laughed a few times on the drive home.

That laugh had stuck in his memory, mostly because he personally hadn't found much of anything amusing after his conversation with Jenny Dalton, the principal of the elementary school and Seth Dalton's wife.

There was another woman who apparently thought he was doing a lousy job taking care of the girls. Oh, she had been kind enough when she gently asked if he needed any help Christmas shopping for the girls.

What, did she think he was going to leave their stockings empty, for crying out loud?

And then she had just as gently asked him if he would mind if she and her daughter Morgan, one of Claire's friends, took her shopping for new clothes during the Christmas vacation.

He looked out at the ranch, his face burning all over again. Apparently, Claire had hit a growth spurt and he had been too busy trying to survive all the changes in his world that he hadn't even noticed. Her parka was a couple inches too short at the wrists and the jeans she told him she and her mother had bought only that summer for back-to-school now looked like floods on her.

While he wasn't paying attention, she was growing tall and slender, just like Suzi had been.

He should have noticed. Instead, someone else had been forced to point out the obvious. A Dalton, no less, even if Jenny was only a Dalton by marriage.

For one dicey moment, he had wanted to tell her to go to hell. But as he watched his oldest niece talking with Morgan and with Tallie, he had been forced to admit she was right. Claire looked like a raggedy urchin and Tallie wasn't much better.

He could afford entirely new wardrobes. Money wasn't the issue, since he had saved virtually all his combat pay the past dozen years and had built a healthy nest egg.

But what he knew about girls' clothing could just about fit inside that dust speck on the inside of the glass.

Under the best of circumstances, shopping wasn't his favorite activity. He had done most of the girls' Christmas shopping online and had found other gifts their parents had left them hidden in the back of the master bedroom closet.

Just the idea of an hour or two at the mall made him break out in a cold sweat.

He didn't miss the irony. He had spent more than a dozen years parachuting into hot spots around the world, packing around seventy pounds of gear as he faced down enemy combatants, constantly aware that he was only a mistake away from going home in a body bag.

But the idea of browsing the shelves of a department store for girly stuff made his palms itch and the hair on the back of his neck prickle.

He needed help. That was the hard, nasty truth, and was most of the reason he stood here gazing out at Emery's cabin and trying to gather his nerves.

Some things a man just wasn't qualified to handle on his own. If Joanie hadn't taken off, he would have dragged her into this. And if Jenny Dalton wasn't married to Seth, he probably would have taken her up on her offer.

But Joanie wasn't here and Jenny wasn't a viable option. He knew what he had to do. His gaze flicked again to the light coming from the window of the cabin, casting its tiny, warm glow against the December night.

He just needed to suck it up, he supposed, and get to it.

Emery Kendall was the most put-together woman he had ever met. From her tasteful earrings to her endless scarves to the tailored cut of her shirts, it was obvious she knew clothes and accessories. Even after she had spent the other night sleeping on his couch and then had chased two girls around the house decorating and making cookies and soup and otherwise spreading holiday cheer, she had looked composed and beautiful.

She would know just the things Claire needed, and Tallie, as well.

If he could think of anyone else to ask for help, he would do it, rather than have to face Emery again after that stunning kiss.

But he was drawing a complete blank here and didn't know what the hell else to do. Since the only other option was to wing it on his own and spend a day making a complete disaster of things in the girls section of Nordstrom's, he supposed swallowing his pride was a small price to pay.

With a strange mix of resignation and dread, he checked on Tallie and Claire to make sure they were soundly sleeping then shrugged into his coat and headed out into the night.

How was it possible for one woman to create such chaos in only a few hours?

Emery looked around the cabin and frowned at the mess. Scraps of fabric covered every surface, she had knocked over a box of ribbon spools and had been too busy to pick them up again, crumpled sketchbook pages had been discarded everywhere and the various shears she was forever losing peeked out from the oddest places.

When her creative muse was upon her, she completely lost track of time and space. She always intended to be so methodical, so careful. But then her mind would race with ideas and before she knew it, her workroom ended up in this complete shambles.

The process of decorating the ranch house with Tallie and Claire the day before seemed to have turned on the spigot of her creative juices. Now she couldn't manage to shut them off.

First thing that morning, as soon as she heard the squeal of brakes on the school bus and realized the canyon had been plowed, she had driven into Idaho Falls. The fabric store options were rather limited there, but between what she found and what she had already brought along of her own designs, she had made huge strides in her plans for the Spencer Hotels project.

She had more than enough for her meeting after Christmas with Eben Spencer and the designer working on his Montana property.

Once she was on a roll, she couldn't seem to stop. She had sewn up a dozen charming ornaments for the rather scraggly little tree she had purchased in town. She had made two tree skirts, one for her little tree and a much larger one for the ranch house, then she had stitched several stockings and now she was throwing together a couple of cloches for the girls.

And she had another idea, one she would have to talk to Nate about. If he agreed, she could give the girls something truly memorable for Christmas. It would take hours of work, just about every available moment she had between now and Christmas, but she was almost positive she could pull it off in the few remaining days.

If he agreed, anyway.

She shouldn't get involved any more than she already was. She knew it perfectly well, but somehow the girls had wormed their way into her heart and she couldn't help wanting to do whatever she could to ease their pain, even just a little.

Ideas and patterns danced across her mind as she went

through the comforting, mechanical motions of working the sewing machine, something that had brought her peace since the first little Singer she'd begged for when she was Tallie's age, sewing her own Barbie clothes.

Finally, the ideas were flying at her so quickly she had to move away from the sewing machine and pick up her sketchbook. She had just begun to make a few rough lines on the paper when the doorbell suddenly rang.

Drat. And double drat.

She thought about ignoring it, about returning to this idea that suddenly seemed so ripe with possibilities. But that wasn't really an option, she supposed. Who else would be stopping at her cabin door but Nate or one of the girls? Since Tallie and Claire ought to be in bed this late on a school night, she could only guess it was Nate.

Her breathing seemed to quicken and she couldn't stop thinking about the taste of him and the hard strength of his arms around her, that kiss that had haunted her memory for the past twenty-four hours.

All the more reason not to open the door.

But he knew she was in here. Her rental vehicle was out front and all the lights were blazing. Somehow she knew the blasted man would only continue ringing the bell until she answered, so it was absurdly self-indulgent to leave him standing out there all night.

But, oh, she was tempted.

Sure enough, the doorbell rang again. She sighed and set her sketchbook facedown and covered it with a fabric swatch for good measure, then she drew in a breath and reached for the doorknob.

He blinked a little when she pulled open the door. She must look a sight, she suddenly realized, with her hair pulled up out of her way in a haphazard knot and the reading glasses she wore for close sewing work on a chain around her neck.

"I'm interrupting."

Yes. "No," she lied. "Come in."

Despite all the clamoring of her instincts, she held the door open for him. He walked inside and his eyes widened further.

"Wow. Looks like a dress shop imploded inside here."

She shrugged. "Something like that. Every once in a while I find my groove and I can't seem to stop."

"I saw your lights on late last night."

The idea of him looking out from the ranch house to her cabin gave her an odd, jittery feeling inside. Had he been thinking about their kiss, too?

I'm a pretty basic kind of guy. I'm afraid my powers of imagination won't stretch quite that far. I don't think I'll be forgetting it anytime soon.

"Ideas started coming after…after yesterday with the girls." *After you kissed me senseless,* she thought, but of course didn't say.

He raised a skeptical eyebrow at the fabric samples spread out everywhere. "Is that a good thing?"

Despite the nerves jumping through her like little frogs on a summer night, she managed to smile. "In this case, it was a very good thing. I have a big presentation right after the holidays for a hotel I'm helping decorate. My idea well has been a little dry lately so I was relieved to make some progress. And then when I was happy with the designs I came up with for that project, the ideas still kept coming."

She moved aside a swatch of folded chintz until she found what she was looking for. "That reminds me. These are for you and the girls."

She held out the three stockings she had made for them, but he didn't reach for them, only stood staring at her. "You made Christmas stockings for us? Why?"

Emery shrugged, feeling foolish. "Impulse. I thought maybe the girls might like new ones for a new start."

He took them, his features still astonished. Though she had chosen a bold green-and-gold striped damask for them, they still looked ridiculously delicate and frilly in his dark, masculine hands. She had embroidered their names on the top cuff in a straightforward serif font.

"You really made these? For us?"

As if she knew any other Tallulahs, Claires or Nates. She flushed and began picking up and carefully folding some of the swatches, simply to have something to occupy her hands. "If you don't like them or if the girls don't, you don't have to keep them."

"I'm stunned. I don't know what to say."

She snapped out a length of jacquard in her own design. "Don't say anything. It's a gift for the girls."

She paused, her hands smoothing the texture of the weave. "You might have noticed we didn't have any stockings hanging yesterday while we were putting up the Christmas decorations."

"I did. I just figured you hadn't found them in the boxes."

"We did, almost right away. But Claire became upset when she saw them—four matching stockings with their names and their parents' names on them. It seemed painful to her to hang those empty stockings, or worse, to just put up their two and leave the other two in the box, so I thought a completely new start might be good for them. But I promise, you won't hurt my feelings if you think they would rather use their old stockings for tradition's sake."

A muscle flexed in his jaw and he cleared his throat. "No. These are great. Really nice. How did you do the names?"

"I have an embroidery stitch on my machine. It's not that hard."

"Well, thank you. Really. Thanks."

"You're welcome. Here, let me put them in a bag for you in case it's still flurrying. You probably don't want them to get wet." She forced her voice to be brisk as she took the stockings from him again and dug through another pile of material until she found a plastic sack from the fabric store.

He lapsed into silence and all those tangled knots in her stomach returned. She held the bag out to him.

"Here you go," she said.

He reached for the bag and as their hands touched, a spark jumped from his fingers to hers. His dark gaze flashed to hers and those knots pulled tighter at the flare of hunger she saw in his eyes.

"Was there something you needed?" she asked, then was mortified at the throaty note in her voice, especially when she was almost certain his gaze shifted to her mouth for just a heartbeat before he jerked it back to meet hers and veiled his expression.

"Actually, yes," he finally said and she didn't miss the slight shadow of hesitation in his voice. "I came to ask a favor, but it seems presumptuous now, after you've gone to all this work already for the girls."

"That was really nothing. It only took me an hour, I promise, and I enjoyed it. Go ahead and ask your favor."

He sighed. "I wouldn't drag you into this if I had another choice. Let me just throw that out there up front."

"Okay," she said slowly, not sure whether to be offended or relieved.

"I had a talk with the principal of the elementary school today."

She waited, but he didn't seem inclined to add more. "Is one of the girls having trouble in school?" she guessed.

"Academically, no. They're both doing okay in that area. Better than I ever did, that's for sure. But the principal seems to agree with you that I'm neglecting them."

She glared at him. "When did I ever say you were neglecting them?"

"Not in so many words, maybe."

"Not in *any* words. Why would I say it when I certainly don't believe it? And neither should this principal! What is he talking about?"

"He's a she. And in this case, Jenny's right. Claire is desperately in need of some new school clothes. Everything she has is worn-out or too small. Tallie's wardrobe isn't much better, but she at least has her sister's hand-me-downs to fall back on."

"What did she suggest?"

"She offered to take Claire shopping, but I didn't feel right about it. I'm their guardian so it's my responsibility." He looked about as thrilled by this particular responsibility as an ant faced with moving a dump truck full of seed pods.

"I noticed a few nice shops in Idaho Falls when I was buying fabric this morning," she said, trying to put as much encouragement in her words as she could muster.

"So you'll do it?" he said quickly.

She blinked. "Do what? You want me to shop for the girls?"

"It would help me more than I can ever repay."

"You're their guardian," she pointed out. "You just said

it's your responsibility. What's the difference between the principal taking Claire shopping and me doing it?"

He frowned. "Okay. None. But training bras and that sort of thing are a little outside my area of expertise. I thought maybe you could just pick up some things and I could give them to the girls for Christmas."

That would be the easy way out for all of them. Given the tension between them and the kiss she couldn't forget, she was no more eager to spend an afternoon in his company than he was to scour the stores for the girls.

"You're going to have to figure it out sometime."

He sighed. "I know. Just like I've had to figure out how to put hair in braids and make more than just ramen noodle soup for dinner and spray the monsters under Tallie's bed with Suzi's patented anti-monster spray. I just thought in a few years the girls will want to do their own shopping anyway, won't they?"

"What's the saying about taking a man fishing versus teaching him to fish? Unless you're planning to get married in the next month or two, someone's not always going to be around to bait the shopping hook for you, Nate."

He looked disgruntled. "You won't help me unless I endure the torture right alongside you, will you?"

She shook her head. "Sorry."

His eyes narrowed and she might have thought he was annoyed if not for that spark she could see there. She was absurdly conscious again of her loose updo and the glasses she had at least pulled off so they hung around her neck on their chain as if she were some sort of flustered librarian.

"Since you're not giving me a choice, I suppose we might as well get this over with. Are you free tomorrow while the girls are in school? They've only got two school days left before Christmas vacation."

She tried to picture a day spent with Nate Cavazos doing something so domestic as shopping for clothes and those knots inside her became a hopeless tangle.

"I'm sure I can drag myself away from my fabric for a few hours."

"Thanks, Em. About nine-thirty work for you?"

She was so flustered at his shortened use of her name that it took her a moment to reply. "Yes. Nine-thirty should be fine."

"Thanks. I'm saying that entirely too often to you lately, aren't I?"

Since it was a rhetorical question that didn't require an answer, she only smiled and opened the door for him.

After he left with the bag of stockings, the cabin seemed quiet and a little forlorn.

That was only the mess, she told herself as she bustled around trying to making a little order out of the chaos. It certainly had nothing to do with a dark-eyed soldier or the memory of his mouth devouring hers.

Chapter Eight

He would rather be standing in the middle of a damn Al-Asra sandstorm than the girls' clothing aisle at Dillard's.

The woman was insane. Why the hell would two young girls need all this stuff? So far she had him carrying three shopping bags crammed to overflowing with sweaters, shirts, slacks, shoes, skirts, underwear and those dreaded training bras.

"How are they both on pajamas?" she asked.

"No idea," he was forced to admit.

"Why don't we start with three pairs each, on the assumption they've got some at home they can still wear?"

"Sounds fine." He had never been a pajama wearer, but had started since he had come back to Pine Gulch. While it had been fine to sleep in skivvies in the army, it didn't feel quite right with two young girls in the house.

"And if you don't mind a suggestion, my...parents

always gave me a new nightgown on Christmas Eve so I had something new when my grandparents descended on Christmas morning."

He had heard that hesitation before when she spoke of her parents and he wondered about it. Had they left behind some kind of bitterness?

Maybe they had more in common than he thought, if that were the case. Heaven knows, he had enough bitterness toward his mother to fill a C-130.

She held up two nightgowns that looked basically the same to him except one was plain red and the other plaid. "Which one?" she asked.

As if he gave a…

"You pick," he tried for diplomacy. "You're better at this than I am."

"You're going to have to shop for them eventually, you know. I'm not going to be here next time they need pajamas."

The thought of life at the ranch after she left gave him a funny, hollow feeling in his gut he decided he was probably wiser not to examine too closely.

"Why don't you get one of each? The plain one in Claire's size and the plaid for Tallie?"

"Good choice," she answered with a smile. "I think that should just about do it, unless you can think of anything else for Christmas you need to buy while we're in town? Stocking stuffers? Christmas dinner?"

"I haven't given that much thought," he admitted.

It *would* be a relief to wrap up the whole shebang today and be done. Except for putting together any items that might need assembling. And wrapping. And shoving all this stuff under the tree on Christmas Eve. And fumbling through Christmas dinner.

"It's harder than I ever dreamed, taking care of all the details," he confessed.

Her eyes softened at what he was suddenly afraid sounded like desperation in his voice. She rested a hand on his forearm and squeezed gently and he was intensely aware of her. "You'll figure things out, Nate. Right now everything seems new and overwhelming, I would guess. Once you get into a routine, it will probably all seem easier."

He wanted to bask in that concern in her eyes, the warmth of her skin that penetrated even through his jacket and shirt.

Too quickly, she removed her hand and he wondered why her cheeks looked a little more pink than usual.

He thought of all her hard work on those stockings and realized he needed something good to fill them. "I haven't given stocking stuffers much thought."

"Hmm." She pursed her lips. "What about a nice journal or some jewelry, since they both have pierced ears?"

"That sounds good."

"Or some things for their rooms, maybe."

"Again, I'll defer to your wisdom."

They walked to the jewelry counter and she helped him select a couple earring assortments for each of them, as well as some delicate necklaces with angels on them. Emery was so excited when she saw them and he couldn't help remembering the conversation he had overheard while they were making cookies, and Tallie's cynicism.

They spent another half hour looking for smaller items until she finally declared herself satisfied with their choices.

The checkout line was already long with similarly over-burdened shoppers, but Emery didn't seem to mind.

"I had an idea, actually, for a gift I would like to make for the girls," she said as they took their place behind a woman carrying only two bags instead of the three he held. "I meant to talk to you about it last night when you stopped by, but I didn't have a chance."

"You don't have to make them anything. I think you've done enough already."

"I know I don't *have* to." She smiled again and he thought how bright and lovely she became when she smiled, not at all like the stiff, elegantly detached creature he had thought her when she first arrived at the ranch. "It's a nervy suggestion and you might not like it, but it's something I'd really like to do."

"I'm all ears now," he said drily.

"The other day when I was helping the girls decorate the little trees in each of their bedrooms, I couldn't help noticing their comforters were nice, but they were starting to wear out. Not much, just a little. Textiles are my business so of course that's the first thing I see."

"It's about the last thing I pay attention to," he confessed. "I'm afraid I haven't noticed anything wrong with their comforters."

"I was thinking I would like to make a couple of quilts for their beds. I sketched out the patterns for them and everything…and then I thought, wouldn't it be wonderful if I pieced them using familiar clothing of their parents? A favorite dress of their mother's, maybe some ties or T-shirts of their father's. You haven't thrown away all of Suzi's and John's clothing, have you?"

He shook his head. "I had Joanie box it all up, but everything is still in the master bedroom. I keep thinking I need to take it all to Goodwill. Maybe after the holidays."

"Would you mind if I looked through the boxes and took some of the things to cut up for them?"

"It's three days before Christmas. How could you possibly finish a project like this by then?"

"I wouldn't have time to hand stitch them," she acknowledged. "But I'm a fast machine quilter. I know I can do it."

That she would even suggest such a project astonished him. The woman barely knew the girls, but she wanted to spend endless frenzied hours on a gift he knew both Tallie and Claire would find beyond price.

"You're supposed to be on vacation!"

"Working vacation, remember?" She smiled. "Anyway, this is what I love to do, Nate. Since I accomplished so much yesterday on my most pressing project, I've got plenty of time. I want to do this, if you'll let me. Please?"

He studied her, the sincerity and the hope in her eyes. She made him want to borrow a little of that hope himself and believe for a little while that everything would be okay.

"How can I say no, especially when the clothes would only go to a secondhand store somewhere? I know the girls would treasure such a gift, if you're sure this is something you really want to do."

"Positive." She smiled radiantly, brighter than the sun reflecting off the brilliant snow outside, but then it was their turn at the checkout counter so she dropped the subject.

By the time they paid for their purchases and left the mall, his feet ached in his boots as if he had marched twenty kilometers across the desert, his bank account had seen a substantial dent and he was ravenous.

"I owe you at least lunch for all this," he said after they had loaded the packages into the cargo space of his SUV.

"To tell you the truth, I'm so excited to get started on the quilts, I can hardly wait to go back to the ranch. But I suppose we have to eat."

"How do you feel about Mexican?"

"Love it!" she said, and he wondered again what put that color in her cheeks.

He took her to one of his favorite authentic Mexican restaurants in town, still around from his high school days. Over hot, salty chips and fresh-made salsa heavy on the cilantro, they talked about mostly inconsequential things—the ranch and her shop in Virginia and her plans for the Montana project. After their server brought their food and set it down with the warning that the plates were hot, as if they couldn't figure that out from the nuclear-reactor-type hand mitts she used, he finally asked the question that had been burning through him for days.

"Why are you here, Em?"

Surprise flickered in her gaze and something else, something almost furtive. "I'm having what looks like a really great chicken quesadilla."

"You know I don't mean here at Lupe's. I mean here in Idaho. Who comes to the middle of nowhere to be alone for the holidays? I know there's more of a story here. You told me you were divorced, but what about family? Aunts, uncles, cousins? Why would you choose to be alone?"

She took a sip of her raspberry lemonade, avoiding his gaze. "I...don't really have any family. My parents were both only children. My mother died in September after being diagnosed with non-Hodgkins lymphoma two days before Christmas last year. My...father died a few years before that."

She was evading the question and he still wondered why. "No significant other in the picture?"

"I haven't really dated anyone since the divorce. My mother's cancer diagnosis a year ago sort of took center stage in my life."

Maybe that was the reason she wanted to be alone. Maybe she still hadn't gotten over her cheating ex. He didn't like to think about her marriage. And because it bugged him, he decided to probe further. Sort of like the time he'd been hit by a sniper in Kirkuk during an engagement and for weeks after had hung that dented Kevlar above his bunk so he could look at it every night before he crashed.

"Even if you wanted the divorce, I imagine it's still tough to close the book on a marriage you probably thought would last forever."

She gazed at him, shock widening the blue of her eyes, then released a soft sigh. "Yes. It has been difficult. But not for the reasons you might think. It wasn't the divorce itself so much as…everything else."

She was quiet for a long moment, then she let out a breath, fidgeting with her napkin.

"I told you my husband cheated," she spoke in a rush. "I didn't tell you he had his little affair with a coworker while I was pregnant with our first child."

What kind of bastard would even consider looking at another woman while his own extraordinarily lovely wife grew big with his child? Nate uttered a couple of pungent military words out of pure disgust at the man.

Her short laugh sounded surprised, but not offended, much to his relief since he hadn't realized he'd cursed aloud.

"Excellent analysis, considering you've never met him," she said.

"What can I say? I'm a keen judge of character."

She smiled in return, but it quickly faded. "I was not quite six months pregnant when Jason told me he was leaving me for her on Christmas Eve two years ago, on the way home from dinner with my mother," she said after a long moment. She spoke the words dispassionately, but he sensed far more emotion stored behind her words than she allowed to seep through.

"Merry Christmas."

"Right. We were on a snowy road and I was driving. In my shock and confusion and, well, fury, I guess, I became distracted and I wasn't paying proper attention to the road. We slid on a patch of ice and hit a tree."

He swore again, more gently this time, somehow sensing what came next.

"I broke my arm and a few ribs, that was all. Nothing really serious. Jason only had a concussion, I'm sorry to say."

He would have smiled at that, if not for the anguish in her eyes. "But…the airbag deployed and I went into premature labor. My daughter only survived a few hours and died just before midnight Christmas Eve. She was three and a half months early and just too fragile to survive such a trauma."

He stared at her, stunned at the sorrow she had endured. How could he have thought her cold when she first arrived at the ranch? It was all a smokescreen, just the fancy veneer she wrapped around all this pain.

A lump rose in his throat and he wanted to pull her into his arms and hold on tight. Since this didn't seem quite the place for that, amid the bustle of waiters and the cooks in the open kitchen talking loudly to each other in Spanish, he settled for picking up her hand and lifting it to his mouth.

It was an uncharacteristic gesture for him, but it somehow seemed just right. "I am truly sorry, Em."

She looked flustered, but didn't pull her hand away. "I guess you can see why Christmas isn't my favorite holiday. The past few haven't been the greatest. Three years ago, my…father died just a week before Christmas, my mother was diagnosed with cancer last year just a few days before Christmas. And between those particular events, I spent the Christmas two years ago in a medicated haze amid the ruins of my life."

She finally withdrew her hand and folded it with the other one in front of her. "This year I just wanted to escape it all. The memories and the heartache and the craziness."

"And then I put you in a position where you couldn't avoid it. First by decorating the house then Christmas shopping with me today." He remembered their conversation earlier and suddenly frowned. "And the quilts. The last thing you need to be doing is taking on such a huge Christmas project like making quilts for Tallie and Claire. It's a great idea, but maybe I can find someone in town to do it after the holidays."

"Not on your life!" she exclaimed. "I want to do this for them, Nate."

"Are you sure?"

"Positive. Working at my sewing machine is cathartic for me, I promise."

He was about to argue when he suddenly heard someone calling their names.

"Nate Cavazos! And Emery! Hello."

He turned and found Wade and Caroline Dalton approaching their table with bright smiles, carrying a couple of doggie bags. They must have been seated in the other dining room of the restaurant or he would have seen them when Nate and Emery came in.

He couldn't quite figure out their warmth toward him. He'd done nothing to encourage it, but since he'd been back in Pine Gulch, they had never treated him with anything but open friendliness.

He ought to be able to see beyond the surface resemblance, but every time he saw Wade Dalton, he saw Hank, big and handsome and commanding.

Caroline Dalton reached her hands out to squeeze Emery's. "How are you? It's so lovely to see you again!"

"Emery was kind enough to help me finish some last-minute shopping for the girls," he said. He wasn't sure he liked the speculative gleam in her eyes.

Wade gave him a commiserating sort of look. "Shopping, huh? Misery loves company, I guess. I was dragged along today, too, mostly to be the sherpa, I think. Though I can't imagine someone climbing Mt. Everest needed to carry more stuff than this."

Caroline rolled her eyes. "We have four children, Wade, and multiple nieces and nephews. The packages tend to pile up." She turned back to Nate. "I'm sure you're finding that, aren't you, even though you've only got two?"

"Right," Nate replied.

Emery said nothing and he suddenly realized with consternation that in the past few moments, all the bright animation on her features had drained away and her mouth was drawn into a tight line.

Why? He thought of her intention to retreat from the craziness of the holidays. Maybe she didn't like Caroline Dalton's reference to their close-knit family and the craziness of it, since she had none of that.

"Are you both coming?"

He jerked his attention back to the conversation. "Coming?"

"To the party tomorrow night at the McRavens."

Oh, right. The party he was supposed to RSVP to, the one he'd completely forgotten.

"I know the children are so excited about it. The girls love swimming at the McRavens. You'll be there, right? And Emery, you, too."

"I don't…"

"You might as well say yes," Wade said with a broad smile to Emery that somehow only seemed to deepen those shadows in her blue eyes. "She's just going to keep badgering you until you agree."

"I am not," Caroline protested. "I asked nicely. Of course, I'm not taking no for an answer. Tomorrow night, seven o'clock. We'll see you both there, and the girls, as well."

With one last bright smile and wave, Caroline towed her husband toward the door, leaving an awkward silence in their wake.

"Why don't you like the Daltons?" Nate finally asked when the silence had drawn on for several beats too long.

Her gaze flashed to his and he saw a furtive flicker there for just a moment before she became serene and composed once more. "Why would you think I don't like them?"

"I don't know. Just a vibe. You don't seem any more thrilled at the party invitation than I am. Am I wrong?"

She pursed her lips. "I like them well enough," she said slowly. "We've only met once and Caroline was nothing but kind to me."

"But you still don't want to go."

Again that mysterious *something* glimmered in the depths of lovely blue eyes that reminded him of someone.

Tell me, he wanted to say. He almost thought she was going to. She opened her mouth and drew in a little breath then closed it again.

"I wasn't expecting to socialize when I came to Pine

Gulch," she answered, twirling her fork through the food she had barely touched. "I'm not part of your community. Why on earth would they even want me at their neighborhood Christmas party when I'm definitely not part of the neighborhood, especially when I'm only here until the end of the week?"

He knew damn well he shouldn't have this little clutch in his gut at the thought of her leaving, at how empty he knew Hope Springs would feel when she was gone. Before he could come up with an answer, she turned the tables back on him.

"What about you? What's your objection to the Daltons as neighbors?"

He didn't want to bring up the whole sordid past, but he couldn't completely lie to her, either. Not when she had shared such painful pieces of her life with him.

"Our families have a somewhat…tangled history."

"Oh?" She set down her fork and gave him an oddly intent look.

"Long story," he answered. One he wasn't about to delve into right now with her. As far as he was concerned, it was all in the bitter past and he hated remembering it.

He glanced at his watch in a lame attempt to change the subject. "Do you want a box for that? You haven't eaten much, but we should probably wrap this up if we want to make it back to the ranch in time to hide the goods before the girls' bus shows up."

"I don't need a box. It was delicious, but I'm finished."

So much for their pleasant lunch, he thought as he helped her into her coat. Secrets and grief and the Daltons all in one convenient package.

It was enough to sour him on Lupe's for a long time.

Chapter Nine

This had all been a terrible mistake.

Not just the day spent with Nate, though she had a sinking feeling she would have an even more difficult time extricating herself from his and the girls' world after today.

But coming to Idaho in the first place had been a foolish, rather pathetic attempt to forge a connection that didn't exist.

Coming here, meeting the Daltons, had seemed like such a good idea back in Virginia, wrapped in the familiar safety of home and still reeling from grief and shock after her mother's death. She had no one else, and this fragile connection had seemed the only thing she had to hang on to.

Mostly she had been curious about them. What kind of men were the Dalton brothers? Were they happy? Healthy? Did they treat their families kindly?

She never expected everything to become so tangled.

The truth was, just as she had told Nate, she was an outsider here and nothing would change that. And hadn't she spent enough time feeling like an outsider, even in her own family?

Her mother and father loved her. She had never doubted that. But they preferred to show that love from a distance, in between Junior League meetings and rounds of golf and social engagements.

Coming here changed nothing, except maybe to reinforce how alone she was.

"Don't worry."

She blinked at Nate across the width of his SUV. "Sorry?"

"That frown of concentration. You look like you're scared to death I'm going to spin out and drive into a ditch. Relax. We're okay. The roads aren't slick. Besides, I've been driving in snow since I was fourteen."

"Except the years when you were driving in sand."

He smiled. "True enough."

She looked out the window and now that she wasn't lost in thought, she realized snow whirled around the vehicle and a few inches had piled onto the road while they had been shopping and having lunch.

"I'm not worried," she said, forcing a smile.

"Lie."

Not about the snow. "I'm sorry. I didn't realize you have a built-in polygraph unit in here."

"Don't need one. I can tell these things."

As she couldn't tell him the real reason for her frown, that she was regretting ever stepping foot in Pine Gulch, she decided to let him believe what he wanted. "All right. Distract me from the snow. Tell me what it was like to grow up in Idaho and why you're not thrilled to be back."

That last had been a shot in the dark, but the sudden tightness around his mouth confirmed her hunch.

He shrugged. "I couldn't wait to leave. I enlisted in the army the moment I was old enough for them to take me and I haven't looked back."

"Why?"

"Lots of reasons," he said, then added somewhat reluctantly, "most of them ugly."

She said nothing, waiting for him to tell her if he wanted. If he didn't, she respected his privacy enough not to pry. Heaven knows, she had enough secrets of her own.

For a long moment, the only sound in the vehicle was the swish of the wipers beating back the flakes and the tires whirring on the road.

Finally he sighed. "My dad died when I was ten. He had an aneurysm and drove his pickup off a steep embankment."

He said the words without emotion, but she heard the quiet sorrow behind them anyway and her heart squeezed. "Oh, Nate. I'm sorry."

He shot her a quick glance, but quickly turned his attention back to the road in order to slow down as they approached the turn into Cold Creek Canyon.

"Ten is a tough age for a kid to lose his dad, especially when, well, my mother wasn't exactly stable."

Again, she remained silent, allowing him to decide how much he would tell her.

"My mother didn't do well on her own."

"Some women don't."

"Right. She was definitely one of those women. She… had her first affair about two months after my dad died. With a married man. A neighbor. I'm sure he offered her sympathy and a willing ear. Maybe advice around the ranch. Whatever. But because she was romantically involved with him, the bastard was able to cheat her out of some valuable pasture land along the river and a healthy portion of my dad's estate before he dumped her. I'm sure he would have taken the whole thing if he could have figured out a way."

"What did your mother do?"

His laugh was short and humorless. "She didn't take their break up well. That's an understatement. She was already depressed and I think she had been teetering on the brink of instability even before my father died. But when that bastard Da… When he dumped her, it sort of threw her over the edge. She started drinking heavily, sleeping with half the men in town. And not discreetly, either."

"Oh, Nate."

"I didn't mind so much for me, but it was tough on my sister to watch. The more my mother would drink, the more she slept around and the more she hated herself. The more she hated herself, the more she drank and slept around. It was an endless cycle."

"What happened to her?" she asked, though she was suddenly loath to hear the answer.

"When I was fourteen, she ran off with a trucker who came through town. Suzi was twenty-one. My sister dropped out of college in Pocatello and came back to run the ranch and get me through high school. Linda died a few years later. She was shot in a convenience store hold-up in Texas, which might seem like one of those genuinely unfair tragedies, except it was her current twenty-three-year-old boyfriend holding up the store."

She couldn't imagine how difficult that all must have been for him, a young man trapped in his mother's downward spiral, forced to watch her throw away her life with promiscuity and alcohol abuse.

"I guess you see why I feel so obligated to the girls," Nate went on as he drove under the Hope Springs arch. "My sister gave up her whole life to come back to Pine Gulch and raise me, rather than let me go into foster care. Suzi wanted to be a teacher, but she left school short only a couple semesters."

"I'm sure she had a good life here even without her degree. She and her husband were building something beautiful at Hope Springs. The guest ranch, the girls. Everything. I didn't know her, but I can only believe she was happy with her life by the love and care she poured into the house and her daughters."

A muscle worked in his jaw. "Well, even though I might hate Pine Gulch and want nothing more than to be back with my platoon, I feel like I have no choice but to do the same for Suzi's daughters that she did for me."

She thought of the men she knew back in Virginia, career-oriented, focused, driven. How many of them would be willing to give up what they loved most and enter a completely foreign situation in order to pay a debt of honor?

Few, if any. She was quite certain of it.

"They're blessed to have you," she murmured.

He shifted in the seat. "Don't know about that. But right now, none of us has much of a choice."

They drove in silence the remaining few moments until they reached the ranch house and sprawl of outbuildings.

She was in grave danger, she thought as he pulled up at her guest cabin. Her emotions were in turmoil. If she wasn't careful, she just might go careening headlong into love with this hard, dangerous, complicated man.

And wouldn't that just be a mess? She didn't need more

emotional torment in her world right now and falling for Nate Cavazos would only result in heartache for her.

"Where are you going to put everything to hide it from the girls?"

He shrugged. "They're sneaky and they know every inch of the house. I wouldn't be surprised if they've already searched every closet and cubby."

"Where have you hidden everything else?"

"Under the bed in the cabin farthest from the house. It's the one we rent out least often and nobody goes there."

"Very sneaky."

Despite the tension still evident in his tight shoulders after their discussion of his childhood, he managed a lop-sided smile.

"I'm an army Ranger. We're good at sneaky."

She returned his smile, even as she felt that precarious shift and slide of her heart.

"I'll help you hide everything," she said. "You don't have much time before the bus arrives, do you?"

He glanced at his watch. "I should be safe for a half hour or so. But really, you've done more than enough."

"Listen, I didn't spend three hours at the mall for you to mix everything up and forget who gets what. This shouldn't take very long. I'll sort things into separate piles. That way when you're ready to wrap, you won't have such a hard time figuring things out."

He didn't argue, only shrugged and climbed out of the SUV to unlock the cabin closest to the river.

She carried as many bags as she could inside and found this cabin very similar to hers. Hers was a little bigger, but they had the same layout, with one main living area and a separate bedroom and bathroom.

The main difference was in the color and tone of the decor. Her cabin was decorated in mountain chic, with deep reds and blues, while this had a slightly more feminine feeling, with tans and sage and a few lavender accents thrown in.

His sister had a natural flair for decorating, she thought. Both places were warm and restful. She thought again what a shame it would be if Nate decided to close the guest ranch after his sister and her husband had worked so lovingly to create these cozy havens for their guests.

He turned on the electric fireplace and by her second trip inside with more bags, the cabin had warmed considerably.

"I think that's everything," she said when he started to head out to the vehicle again.

He nodded and closed the door to keep out the icy air.

Even though they had just driven thirty miles together in the relatively small space of his SUV, somehow being alone together in the cabin had a different sort of intimacy. She pushed away that insistent awareness. Yes, he was dark and gorgeous and masculine. But he was also off-limits, she reminded herself.

Emery swallowed hard as she carried the last bags into the small bedroom and began sorting their purchases into two piles.

He joined her and the room seemed to shrink until the only things she could focus on were Nate and the big queen bed with the antique brass bedstead.

"When do you intend to wrap everything?" she asked, hoping he didn't notice the way her fingers trembled a little as she sorted.

"I want to get everything out of the way. I was thinking maybe tonight after the girls are asleep."

"Do you need help?"

The moment the words were out, she wanted to drag them back, especially when he raised an eyebrow in surprise.

"An unusual offer for someone trying to avoid Christmas this year."

She couldn't rescind the offer now, as much as she might want to. "I just don't want you to make a mess of all my hard work picking the perfect gifts by shoving them into any old bag. Presentation is half of what makes a good gift."

He snorted. "Maybe for your country club set. But the girls are eleven and eight. Hate to break it to you, but they're going to rip off whatever wrapping paper you put around them in about two-point-six seconds."

She laughed ruefully. "Well, for those two-point-six seconds, presentation is important."

He was silent for a long moment. When she looked up from the sweaters she was sorting, she found him studying her with an odd, intent look in his eyes. "You really need to do that more often, Em."

"Do what?"

"Laugh. It makes you breathtaking."

Before she could catch a single thought through her shock at his words, he brushed his thumb at the corner of her still-uplifted mouth. Her smile slid away and she froze at his touch and the glittery shower of sparks cascading through her.

Her gaze held with his for a long moment and she saw something dark and sultry kindle in his eyes. He leaned forward slightly, his lids half-lowered, but he didn't move those final few inches to press his mouth to hers.

He was leaving the decision to her, she thought, and somehow the discovery made it that much easier to arch across that small space between them and slide into his kiss.

The room was chilly, but his mouth was warm, focused. She wrapped her arms around his neck, vaguely aware she was still holding one of the little angel necklaces she had picked out for the girls.

Their kiss a few nights earlier had been raw and intense, shocking mostly because it had been so unexpected. But they had been building toward this one all day as they had shopped and walked and talked, sharing a meal and confidences and their private pain. It seemed inevitable, somehow, this coming together, like the first fledgling crocuses poking through the snow after a long, hard winter.

Everywhere she touched was solid, hard muscle and she wanted to sink into him.

"You taste like raspberry lemonade," he murmured against her mouth. "Sweet and tart and delicious."

His low words rasped across her skin and she decided she would drink no other beverage for the rest of her life. He deepened the kiss and she tightened her arms around his neck, lost in the wild torrent of sensation.

As they kissed and tasted for long, drugging moments, somehow they shrugged out of their coats, though she had no real awareness of it. A moment later, she could feel his hand at her waist and then the sizzling warmth of his fingers on her bare skin under her sweater.

She wanted him more than she had ever wanted anything in her life, this man with the bedroom eyes and the hard strength.

Their purchases covered just about every inch of the bed, but she didn't care. She wanted to sweep all her carefully sorted piles onto the floor and drag him down. But just as she started to reach behind her with some vague intent of making space for them, the sudden whine of airbrakes in the distance cut through the cold afternoon air.

At the sound, he dragged his mouth away and stared at her, his pupils expanded so that his entire irises looked black and dangerous.

Reality crashed down, harsh and unforgiving. She had completely lost control. Another few moments and she would have lost every ounce of good sense.

What on earth was she thinking? This wasn't her. She didn't have torrid affairs with men she had barely met and would probably never see again a week from now.

She drew in a sharp breath and eased away from him, fumbling to straighten her clothes that had become so disordered in their embrace.

"That must be the school bus." Her voice sounded thready and aroused and she quickly cleared her throat. "I can finish up here and hide everything back under the bed. You had better go meet the girls or they'll be suspicious."

He raked a hand through his hair, looking just as stunned and disoriented as she felt. "Emery..."

"Go. They'll be looking for you."

After a long moment, he picked his coat off the floor and yanked it on, shoved on his Stetson she must have tipped off somehow, then walked out into the cold, leaving a yawning sort of silence behind him.

With mechanical movements, not daring to take a moment to even think about what had nearly happened between them, Emery quickly finished sorting the gifts and shoved them all under the bed with the others, then turned off the heat and closed the door behind her, making sure it locked securely.

When she finally reached her own cabin, she shut the

door and sagged on to the sofa as everything inside her still seemed to tremble and sigh. She could still taste him, still feel that leashed strength under her fingertips.

This heat between them was crazy. Incendiary and fierce and completely out of control. She wasn't used to losing control like that. She liked things to be tidy, orderly. Or at least she always thought she did.

She thought of the chaos of her workspace when she was in the middle of a project. That was the only area of her life where she allowed disarray, since she had learned along the way that she did her most creative work when she just let herself be free and unencumbered by the expectations she always felt pressing down on her.

Maybe that was part of Nate's appeal. He didn't seem to expect her to be perfect.

She pressed a trembling hand to her chest, where her heart still raced. She had to put a stop to this. If she didn't, she was suddenly afraid she would end up leaving Pine Gulch more messed up than when she had arrived.

The girls tag-teamed him about the neighborhood party the minute they bounded up the driveway from the bus stop.

Tallie hit him up first. "Uncle Nate, have you decided if we're going to the party at the McRavens'? It's tomorrow! We have to decide, 'cause we're supposed to MVP or something."

"RSVP," Claire corrected with a "you big dork" tone to her voice. "It's when you tell someone whether you're going to their party so they know if they have enough food for everyone and nobody goes hungry. So are we going?"

"Can we, Uncle Nate? Can we? Huh?" Tallie dropped her backpack in the foyer and threw her arms around him for emphasis. "It will be super fun. Tanner says they're having Christmas carols and games and Santa Claus might even come. We *have* to go. Please say yes."

"We don't *have* to go," he muttered.

"But we *want* to. We really, really want to!" Claire exclaimed, with far more enthusiasm than she usually showed toward anything.

He gave an inward groan, not at all in the mood to tangle with them over this, especially after he was still reeling from the sheer stunning impact of Emery's kiss.

"I still haven't decided," he said firmly. "We can talk about it again after dinner. Meantime, why don't you show me what homework you brought home, then we can all get on to our chores."

Something about his firm tone must have gotten through to them. Or to Claire, anyway. When Tallie would have continued nagging and fretting at him like a puppy working a treat out of a rubber chew toy, Claire elbowed her in the ribs and muttered something in her ear he couldn't hear. Tallie gave a long-suffering sigh, but to his vast relief, she let the discussion drop—for a while, anyway.

She quickly picked it up again after they all came in from finishing their chores in the barn—and after he had made a quick, clandestine stop at Emery's cabin while the girls were busy to drop off the clothing she had asked for.

While he was warming up dinner, one of the prepared freezer meals he purchased from a company in Idaho Falls, Tallie started in.

"We should really let the McRavens know if we're coming to the party," she tried again from the kitchen table where she was supposed to be working on her homework. "Otherwise they might be mad."

"I'm sure they won't be mad."

"But what if they run out of food? Drew says Mrs. McRaven is the best cook. I don't want to miss the food."

"She is a great cook." Claire set aside her history worksheet. "Everybody always buys her cookies and cupcakes first when we have bake sales at school."

"And we can take our swimming suits and everything," Tallie reminded him for about the hundredth time. "On the bus this morning, Kip said they have a brand-new slide that curls around and goes into the deep end. It's gonna be so *awesome*. Don't you think we should call and tell them if we're coming?"

After about fifteen minutes of their pestering, Nate ground his back teeth, suddenly sick of anything to do with the word *party*.

What the hell had happened to his life? Five months ago he had been leading patrols, taking on bad guys, serving his country. Now he spent his days worrying whether the girls were drinking enough milk, whether they finished their math homework, if he had remembered to add the damn fabric softener to the load of whites in the washing machine.

Kissing his guests until he couldn't think straight.

"Look, I said I would think about it," he snapped in a harsh tone he didn't think he'd ever used with them before. "Let it go, both of you, or I'll say no just to shut you both up. Why do you have to hound me and hound me about everything?"

Tallie blinked in surprise and a little bit of fear, he was chagrined to see. She set down her fork beside her half-eaten casserole.

Her chin wobbled a little, but she didn't cry, which made him feel even worse. "I'm not hungry anymore," she said after five more minutes of tense silence.

"Me, neither," Claire looked down at the tablecloth and not anywhere close to his direction. "May we be excused?"

"Yeah," he said shortly. It was their night to wash dishes, but he decided not to push the matter, even though every child behavior specialist would probably tell him he should do exactly that. He'd already been told by Principal Dalton and others that he should do what he could to keep a regular, consistent schedule so the girls could begin to restore a little order and stability in their world.

They scraped their chairs away and he felt about three inches tall when they hurried from the kitchen without another word.

He sat there alone and doggedly finished his casserole even though he wasn't at all hungry, either, then stood and scraped their dishes, wishing Emery were there to talk him through this. She would know how to smooth this over, what he could say to make things right again.

The fact that he found himself wanting to turn to her made him nervous all over again about the impact she was having in their lives.

He sighed as he loaded the last dish in the dishwasher, added detergent and closed the door.

He really needed a housekeeper. With Joanie gone, the house was falling apart and he just didn't have the time to take care of everything and run the ranch, as well. That was right at the top of his list after the holidays.

But first he was going to have to go to the damn party, to smile and make conversation and basically put on a huge show that he was happy to be there.

It was just a party. He wasn't facing interrogation by an enemy combatant. He could be polite for a few hours. Other neighbors would be there besides the Daltons so he wouldn't have to sit and socialize with just them. For that matter, he could probably avoid the lot of them for most of the night.

Through the doorway, he caught sight of the Christmas tree Emery and the girls had decorated. None of them had turned on the lights at dusk so he hurried in and flipped the switch. After a moment of watching the colors reflected in the glass, he felt a little better. He remembered that happiness he had seen in Emery's eyes earlier when she had been talking about making the quilts. This was the season of joy, of hope, and he was acting like the world's biggest Scrooge.

He sighed and headed up the stairs, wondering if the crow he had to eat would taste any better than the casserole he had forced himself to swallow.

He found both girls on Claire's bed listening to her CD player with a headphone splitter.

They both gave him disgruntled looks when he opened the door and guilt poked at him. He sat on the edge of the bed, wondering if this would ever feel more natural.

"Look, guys, I warned you I would be lousy at the whole parenting thing. I don't know what the he—heck I'm doing. I've been straight with you about that. But that's no excuse for me to be mean. I'm sorry about earlier. I don't really want to go to the neighborhood party and I've been trying to come up with some excuse not to go."

They both opened their mouths and he could see arguments brewing in their eyes, but he shook his head to cut them off. "But since this is something you both want to do and since we're a family now and need to work together and compromise when we have to, I'll play nice and somehow make it through."

They both squealed and Tallie threw herself into his arms. "Thank you, thank you, thank you. It's gonna be so fun. You'll see."

Right. He couldn't wait. But at least the girls were talking to him again, so he supposed he could survive.

"Okay, a few more minutes and then it's time for bed. I might not have figured much out about being a parent, but I do know you both need sleep on a school night."

They groaned, but didn't argue with him, much to his relief, since he had an entire cabin full of Christmas presents to wrap.

Chapter Ten

A smart woman ought to be wise enough to stay away from things she knew perfectly well weren't good for her. Things like strawberry cheesecake brownies and sappy movies when she was in a sentimental mood and half-off sales at her favorite designer shoe store.

And gorgeous army Rangers with big, dark eyes and wide shoulders and those impossibly long eyelashes.

Emery sighed, her gaze fixed on the glow coming from the windows of the last cabin in the row. The light had been on for the past half hour and she had stood here that entire time, gazing out the window and trying not to picture the scene.

He had to be wrapping presents for his nieces, ungainly thumbs and all. The idea of him sitting inside there surrounded by ribbons and tape and girly stuff gave her a funny little ache in her chest.

For the past eighteen hundred seconds, she had been

debating the wisdom of walking the distance between them. Yes, she had offered to help him. But then he had kissed her instead of answering.

Didn't that rather negate her offer?

Spending time with Nate in a small, enclosed space would be about as smart as walking barefoot across the thin, crackly ice of Cold Creek, especially after the heat they had shared in that very same cabin just a few hours before.

But she *had* offered. And he *did* need help. She still firmly believed that all those lovely things they bought for the girls would lose some of their magic without proper wrapping and Nate himself had admitted he tended to be all thumbs.

Who was she kidding? Emery released a heavy sigh. He was right, the girls would rip the wrappings off in two seconds. The real truth was, she couldn't seem to stay away from him. Despite all her well-reasoned arguments all afternoon and evening to herself against putting herself in closer to proximity to him, she wanted urgently to walk through the snow to that cabin to spend just a few more moments in his company.

All the more reason she should stay exactly where she was. She didn't come to Pine Gulch with any intention of finding herself entangled with anyone here. Not Nate or the girls, or even the Daltons.

Yet here she was, entangled whether she wanted to be or not.

She already cared for Claire and Tallie and she was wildly attracted to Nate.

What was the big deal if she was attracted to him? He obviously wasn't any more eager than she was to explore this heat between them. He had barely even looked at her a few hours earlier when he dropped off three boxes of clothing he had smuggled out of the house while the girls were busy with chores.

He had been taciturn to the point of rudeness when he told her she shouldn't feel obligated to follow through on her suggestion about the quilts, that he was only dropping off the clothing because she had asked for it. If she didn't want to go to all that trouble, she didn't have to, he assured her.

She had assured him right back that she still wanted to, but he barely even waited around long enough for her response, only said he had to go before the girls spotted him there and became too curious about the boxes.

Emery shifted her gaze from the window to the quilt pieces scattered around every corner of the room.

Heaven knows, she had plenty to do. Even though she had already sketched out both quilts and had started cutting out the pieces, she would be sewing day and night to finish two full-size quilts in three days.

But she could spare a few moments to help him.

She reached for her jacket. She was strong enough to handle any attraction between them. And if *she* wasn't, he would be.

She would just have to trust him. And if a girl couldn't trust an army Ranger who had just spent the day torturing himself by Christmas shopping for his two orphaned nieces, really, who could she trust?

He was making this much harder than it had to be.

Nate looked up from his position at the dining table through the doorway into the bedroom at the massive load of gifts still piled on the bed and the much smaller pile of wrapped presents next to him. The contrast between the two and the reality of how much work he still had to do made him want to bang his head against the chinked wall.

He had switched the little stereo in the cabin to a station playing Christmas carols in the hopes that it might help him get more in the mood for the task.

It wasn't working. He just wanted to bag the whole thing and toss the gifts under the tree as-is on Christmas morning.

Neither of the girls believed in Santa Claus anyway. They had told him so quite solemnly at Thanksgiving when they were watching the Macy's parade on TV instead of the football games he would have preferred.

He didn't need to go to all this fuss and bother. What would be the big deal if he just gave them unwrapped gifts in their stockings?

They would still be getting just as much stuff, after all. And it would sure be easier if he didn't have to try to figure out the proper way to wrap a stupid little tube of lip gloss, for hell's sake.

He picked up a little scrap of discarded silvery paper and rolled it around the tube of candy-flavored lipgloss then ripped a piece of tape off the dispenser and plastered down both ends.

It looked like crap, just like the rest of the presents he had wrapped. But the girls had very few bright spots in their lives right now and Christmas was going to suck enough for them. Maybe the extra time they had to spend unwrapping gifts would help distract them from the gaping void where their parents should be.

He hated thinking about Christmas Eve and Christmas morning, and dreaded how tough it was probably going to be on the girls not to have Suzi and John there watching them open their presents for the first time in their lives.

The first Christmas without their parents needed to be as close to perfect as he could manage. He only regretted that it had taken him until three days before Christmas to figure that out.

He picked up the next gift, a pair of furry pink boots Emery assured him Tallie would love. He was cutting paper to fit the box and listening to a really strange a cappella rendition of "The Little Drummer Boy" when somebody knocked on the door.

For just a moment, panic spurted through him. Had the girls woken up, seen the lights on down here and come to investigate? He was rather frantically looking around for a blanket he could toss over the jumble of presents when he heard a female voice that was definitely neither of the girls.

"Nate? It's me, Emery."

He probably should be relieved the girls hadn't found him, but he was depressed at the realization that his instant of panic didn't ease in the slightest.

"Yeah. Just a minute," he called, sliding his chair away from the table and hurrying to the door.

He opened it for her and told himself that the little leap in his chest at the sight of her, all rosy-cheeked and delectable, was only a little leftover indigestion from the tense dinner with the girls.

"I saw the light. Need a hand?"

He pulled the door open farther so she could enter the cabin. "I wish I could say no. But the truth is, I could use a million hands. Or at least two that know what they're doing here. I really stink at wrapping presents."

She held up her hands. "This is a little-known secret about me, but I majored in advanced ribbon-curling in college."

He laughed, entirely too drawn to this rare teasing side of her. She hadn't worn a coat for the short walk over, only a sweater and a red-patterned scarf wrapped in some complicated way that managed to look elegantly put-together.

He had turned on the electric fireplace when he came down to the cabin, but somehow the room still seemed considerably warmer when she walked inside and began to untwist her scarf.

He could smell her, that alluring scent of cinnamon and vanilla, and he remembered all-too-vividly the taste and heat of her a few hours earlier in this very place. Her curves pressed against him, the sexy little sounds she made when he nuzzled the slender column of her neck, the delectable softness of the skin just above her waist....

"Where would you like me to start?"

He blinked back to the present to find Emery had draped the scarf on the hook by the door and her attention was fixed on the presents piled everywhere.

He scratched the back of his neck, wrenching his mind from that blasted kiss. "I seem to have more trouble with the small stuff. Socks, earrings. Lip gloss. That sort of thing. If you don't mind taking anything smaller than a loaf of bread, I can handle the bigger gifts."

She smiled and he was struck all over again by how lovely she was and how that smile seemed to fill the entire cabin with warmth.

"A very wise and appropriate division of labor."

She gathered up a handful of smaller gifts and one of the rolls of wrapping paper he had been fortunate enough to find in Suzi's stash of holiday stuff, and found a spot on the sofa where she could use the wide coffee table to spread out wrapping paper.

"Do you worry the girls might wake up?" she asked after she was situated and had started wrapping some socks.

"I thought when you knocked at the door I was busted for sure," he admitted.

"Lucky for you it wasn't the girls."

Funny, he didn't feel very lucky when it was all he could do to keep his hands off her. "They both have my cell phone memorized. I also left one of the two-way ranch radios as a backup." He pointed to the matching radio on the kitchen counter.

"You're prepared. Must be your military training."

He gave a rough laugh. "A dozen years in the army wasn't much preparation, I'm afraid, for a night spent wrapping mostly pink girly-girl presents."

"You're doing fine." She smiled.

"I haven't had much practice at this wrapping thing," he admitted. "I usually had the store gift wrap presents for my dad and Suz and my…mom."

She flashed a quick look of sympathy in his direction and he regretted telling her about his childhood. It wasn't a part of his life he liked to broadcast around and he didn't want her looking at him with pity in her eyes.

He would much rather see softness and warmth and…

He jerked his attention from all the things he knew he shouldn't want. He quickly changed the subject. "What about you? You haven't told me much about your family."

She was quiet for several moments while a jazzy piano version of "My Favorite Things" played softly through the cabin. When she spoke, her tone was casual, but somehow he sensed a great importance behind her words.

"My…father was a corporate attorney and my mother

was in public relations. They married after dating in graduate school and I was born not long after."

"And you were an only child, right?"

Again she paused, far longer than the rather benign question warranted. Finally, he looked up from wrapping the pink boots for Claire to find her gazing into the small flames of the electric fireplace.

"Shortly before she died, my mother told me the man I thought all my life was my father really wasn't."

He stared, not knowing what to say. She didn't give him a chance to respond before she continued.

"Apparently, she had a relationship with a married man and I was the result," she went on. "In her family's rather blue blood social circle at that time, illegitimate children still weren't quite acceptable, no matter what the rest of the world might be doing. So when she discovered she was pregnant, her college boyfriend agreed to marry her and raise me as his own. They never said a word in all those years until my mother's deathbed."

Her hands trembled slightly on the wrapping paper and her shoulders were tight and set.

"Whoa," he finally said. "That must have been a shocker."

She gave a ragged-sounding laugh. "You could say that. Apparently, I also have several half-siblings. That's why I didn't quite know how to answer your question. They have no idea about me, at least as far as I know. I'm still trying to figure out if I want to work toward a relationship with them."

He whistled, long and low. "You do play your cards close to your vest, don't you?"

"It's not exactly a story I feel like telling to any stranger passing by. Or to my close friends, for that matter. Actually, you're the only other person who knows I'm not really one of the Kendalls of Kendall Park, daughter of Stephen and Julia Baird Kendall."

He shouldn't feel so flattered that she would confide this part of her life to him. He also shouldn't have the overwhelming urge when he heard that slightly forlorn note in her voice to drop the wrapping paper and tape, fold her into his arms and whisper that everything would be all right.

"You haven't met them?"

She shook her head. "I can't quite figure out how to just show up on someone's doorstep and say, Surprise! I'm your twenty-seven-year-old baby sister."

"That's a tough one."

"The truth is, I'm not sure I'm ready to suddenly parachute into the middle of an instant family."

He couldn't help a little smile at her vivid imagery. "You're right to be cautious. Trust me, that's solid advice coming from someone with experience, literally, at both parachuting and instant families. You don't want to jump into either unless you're a hundred percent sure about the way the wind is blowing, about whether you've got the stomach to make the jump, and about whether you're prepared for what you're going to find on the ground."

"I don't know any of that yet," she admitted as she coiled a ribbon in some elaborate way and adhered it to the package she was wrapping. "I guess that's what scares me most. What am I supposed to do now? I feel like everything I thought I knew about myself has been turned upside down."

"You'll figure it out."

"I hope so." Her voice was small and rather forlorn and his hands tightened on the wrapping paper. He wanted to pull her into his arms, to hold her tight and make all her worries and fears disappear. He wanted to kiss her until that lost look in her eyes began to fade, replaced by the desire he had seen there that afternoon.

He was suddenly afraid this wasn't only about physical attraction. If that was it, why would his insides be jumping around like a grasshopper on a hot July sidewalk?

No, this was more. He genuinely liked this woman. Something about her big blue eyes and her hesitant smile and that indefinable air of loneliness surrounding her reached right in and tugged at his heart.

He was very much afraid these fragile feelings could develop all too easily into something more.

This was tender and gentle and intimate. He wanted to tuck her against him and protect her from anybody else who might want to hurt her.

He didn't *want* this. God knows, he didn't need one more person to worry about. He couldn't handle the life *he* had parachuted into. The last thing he needed was to find himself wrapped up like one of these presents in someone else's troubles.

He ought to just shove her out the door into the cold night and assure her that while he appreciated her help, he could handle wrapping the remaining few gifts on his own.

All of his instincts were crying out for him to do just that, but he forced himself to ignore them.

Still, he sliced through the wrapping paper almost savagely. Damn her for blowing into his world at the most inconvenient time, when he could least afford the distraction and when he found himself in a lousy tactical position to protect himself.

What on earth had she done wrong?

Emery combed through their conversation of the past

ten minutes and could think of nothing she might have said or done to turn his features dark and forbidding, to make that muscle in his jaw clench so tightly.

Was he disgusted that she was the result of an illicit affair? Or did he just not want to be dragged into her problems? In a few moments, he had shifted from offering her advice about parachuting to glowering at the girls' Christmas presents as if he wanted to toss the lot of them out into the snow-covered cattle pens.

They worked in a tense silence, those Christmas carols playing softly between them. Finally, when her pile had considerably dwindled and she only had a few items left to wrap, she decided she'd had enough.

She had spent her entire childhood trying to be perfect, studying hard for the best grades, applying to the right colleges, wearing just the right accessories.

Since her mother died, she had spent some serious time rehashing her life, examining the fierce perfectionism that had carried from childhood into her adult years. Now she could see it for what it was: a rather pathetic effort to gain the approval of a man who had been distant and reserved all her life.

She understood everything so much more clearly now. Stephen Kendall had known she wasn't his biological child all along. Her mother had been clear about that. She could only imagine what he must have seen when he looked at her, another man's child. How could he be expected to give her that love and attention she had craved so desperately?

She had even married the son of one of his law partners to please him. Oh, she might have convinced herself she loved Jason when they started dating in college, but in reality she had been so happy to finally have Stephen Kendall's approval that she could have talked herself into anything.

Somehow she had transferred those efforts to please her father into making herself into the perfect wife, never complaining at Jason's late nights or his unexplained absences. He was working hard at the law firm he'd been folded into after he passed the bar, trying to establish himself so they could continue having their European vacations and their late-model cars and their big brick house in an exclusive neighborhood.

In the midst of all that perfection and despite his past history in college, she had stupidly never once suspected that Jason Markeson would turn out to be a cheating son of a bitch.

She was suddenly tired of it. Hadn't she vowed not to be so passive anymore, to reach out and seize what life had to offer?

"I suppose I have two choices," she finally said and her abrupt statement earned her a rather wary look from Nate.

"About what?"

"I can sit here stewing about what I might have said or done to annoy you. Or I can stop wondering and just outright ask you."

He set aside a large package with a lopsided ribbon. "I'm annoyed?"

"You tell me. If you're not angry, what am I missing? Maybe the glower is just some army commando way of expressing undying gratitude for my help."

"I'm not angry," he said, then added almost under his breath, "Not with you, anyway."

She frowned, a little disconcerted. How narcissistic, she suddenly realized, that she would automatically assume she was the cause of his dark mood. He had stressors she couldn't even imagine, trying to run the ranch and raise his nieces and leave behind the military career he enjoyed.

"Who, then? The girls?"

He let out a long, heavy sigh. "Myself, mostly."

"Why?"

He didn't answer at first and when she met his gaze, she found him watching her with that half-closed look again, something in his dark eyes that sizzled through her insides.

"I don't know what to do about this."

"About…what?"

He sighed. "No matter how many times I tell myself I shouldn't want you, that I don't have time for this, that you're far too proper and polished for a guy like me, I can't seem to help myself."

She stared as that sizzle turned into a full-fledged burn. "Nate…"

"I know. It's crazy, isn't it?"

Her mouth was desert-dry suddenly and she had to force herself to take a deep enough breath to ease the sudden ache in her lungs. "Crazy. Right. Just what I was thinking."

He slid his chair back and the sound startled her into a little jump.

"I can't stop thinking about tasting you, putting my hands on you. All afternoon and evening, I've been wondering what might have happened if we hadn't heard the bus out front earlier."

She swallowed again, her insides hot and restless. "We both know what would have happened," she murmured. "We probably would have ended up on that bed over there."

"Which would have been a mistake for both of us."

"Huge mistake," she agreed.

"Enormous. Colossal."

Even as he said the words, he moved inexorably closer to her and her heartbeat accelerated. Without even being fully conscious of it, she rose.

"But just for the record," she said, her voice low, "I can't stop thinking about you…doing those things, either. I thought you should know."

Her last word was swallowed by his groan and then his mouth was on hers and all the heat from earlier roared back over them as if it had just been lurking between them on a low, steady simmer, ready to flare again.

Right. This felt right. All the reasons and arguments didn't matter when she was here with him, in his arms. She didn't need to be perfect with Nate. He didn't expect that from her and she somehow had a feeling he wouldn't be as attracted to her if he didn't see her for what she was, calluses and scars and all.

He lowered her to the sofa, his body all hard muscle over hers, and she savored the strength of him above her. "I can't get the taste of you out of my head," he murmured, his body stretched along hers. "You're there all the time, no matter what I'm doing."

"I'm sorry."

He laughed roughly. "I'm only sorry the memory of it doesn't do justice to the real thing." He kissed her, his mouth fierce, almost possessive, and she clutched at his back, wondering just how she had come to care so much for this man in such a short time.

She could feel his arousal against her and she arched against him, seeking more. She wanted him, wanted this. The hunger was like a steady wind inside her, sweeping away all her uncertainties.

They kissed and tasted and explored while the soft carols played in the background and she wanted to remember every moment of this forever. He helped her out of her sweater, leaving only the white cotton blouse underneath. When his hands moved to the buttons of her shirt, she reached to help him. With each button that slipped through its opening, he pressed a kiss to the skin exposed.

And then, just as he reached for the last one, when her nerves had reached a fever pitch of anticipation for his touch, the sudden jangle of a cell phone rang through the small cabin.

Chapter Eleven

Both of them froze, their breath ragged. When the phone rang again he swore, low and vicious, wishing he could pound his head against the coffee table a couple dozen times.

"I can't ignore it," he said, fighting a groan. "I want to, more than I want to take my next breath, but I can't."

"I know."

She scrambled up, working the buttons on her shirt with fingers that trembled.

"It's got to be the girls. Claire knows to call me if she can't find me in the house. I always leave the phone by the side of her bed."

"Answer it."

With another quick, muffled curse, he reached for the phone. "What's wrong?"

"Uncle Nate, where are you?" Claire's plaintive cry tore

at his conscience. "Tallie had a nightmare again. A really bad one. She won't stop crying and I don't know what to do."

Walking barefoot out into the snow wouldn't have cooled the intense heat between them any faster. Though it was just about the toughest thing he'd ever had to do, he moved farther away from Emery and reached for his coat.

"I'm outside," he answered, which wasn't technically a lie since he was outside the ranch house.

"Well, can you come back in soon?" she begged. "She's really upset and she just wants Mom and Dad."

"Yeah. Yeah. Of course. I'll be there in a minute."

"Hurry, okay?"

"Hang on, honey. I'm on my way."

She hung up after his assurance that he would be there in a moment. Claire sounded far more composed than he felt. Sometimes he forgot she wasn't twelve yet, that she was still very much a child.

"Don't worry about anything," Emery said as he tucked his shirt back in. "I'll finish up out here and hide the gifts in the bedroom again."

He didn't know what to say that wouldn't make him feel like even more of a heel. "I'm sorry. More sorry than you'll ever know."

Her laugh sounded a little rough, strained. "The girls have excellent timing. First the school bus and now this. It's probably better this way. Neither one of us is in a good place for…anything."

"Em…"

She shook her head. "Go. The girls need you."

He gave her one more regretful look then hurried out into the cold December night.

* * *

An hour later, Nate stood in the darkened great room beside the Christmas tree, watching soft, puffy flakes of snow drift down. Tallie and Claire were finally settled again after a cup of instant hot cocoa and a half dozen stories.

For a good twenty minutes after he rushed to the house, Tallie had sobbed in his arms, distraught from her nightmare. He hadn't done much of anything except hold her and murmur soft little nothing words and promise her repeatedly that he wasn't going anywhere and neither was Claire.

Finally she had drifted back to sleep in his arms and at Claire's suggestion, he had put her in her sister's room in case she woke again.

Was there ever a moment in a parent's life that wasn't touched by guilt? He never should have left the house, even if Claire could reach him quickly on the cell. It wasn't fair that she had to deal with her sister alone in those first few tense moments after Tallie awoke.

Nate sipped at his own lousy powdery mug of hot cocoa then set it on the corner of the mantel. He was exhausted, emotionally and physically, and wanted nothing more than to unburden himself to a willing ear. The lights of Emery's cabin were on and her own little Christmas tree glimmered merrily in the window, but he knew he couldn't leave the house again tonight.

Even if he didn't have to consider the girls, it wouldn't be a good idea to seek her out again.

Too much was at stake. Not just his own increasingly powerful feelings for her, but more important, the girls. Tallie's nightmare was a stark reminder of the psychological trauma his nieces had suffered and how very far they had to go toward healing. Tallie was terrified that everyone she loved would leave her as her parents had done. The grief counselors he'd taken them to said only time and routine would provide the stability she needed.

He knew Emery's place in their world was fleeting. She would be returning to Virginia in a few days and all his instincts urged him to keep her at a distance, for the girls' sake.

But what about *his* sake? He craved her company like a canteen full of pure spring water after a long recon mission in the dessert. She was soft and sweet and when he was with her, he could forget about his worries and the uncertainty of the future and everything he had given up to do what was right for his nieces.

With Emery, he wasn't an ex-Ranger or a greenhorn parent or an out-of-his-league rancher. He was only a man wrapped around a beautiful woman who touched something deep inside him.

He sighed. Probably best that they'd been interrupted before things spiraled out of control, for everybody's sake. Somehow knowing that perfectly well still didn't seem to ease the yearning ache in his gut.

So much for those damn best intentions.

Nate gazed across at the passenger seat of his SUV where Emery sat with her hands folded and her mouth compressed into a thin line.

She looked even more lovely and sophisticated than normal, with her hair swept back into a shiny twist and her makeup so expertly applied, he could hardly tell she was wearing any.

"Why didn't you bring your swimsuit?" Tallie asked her.

"You won't even get cold because the pool's inside the McRavens' house!"

"I believe I've heard that," Emery said drily.

"You should go swimming with us, then!"

"I'll be too busy eating all the good food to go swimming," she said with a smile for the girls that seemed to reach right out and tug at his insides.

He really *had* intended to keep his distance. But he never counted on the girls finding Emery after school at the horse corrals on their daily visits to check on Annabelle, and inviting their guest to ride with them to the party.

A little warning might have been nice. Instead, a few minutes before they were heading out the door, Claire had casually mentioned they needed to pick up Emery because she and Tallie had offered her a ride.

"She said no at first, but we told her it wasn't good for the planet to take two cars," Tallie had confided.

"She couldn't say no after that. I hope it's okay," Claire had said.

It wasn't okay. Bad enough he had to go to the damn party in the first place. Tougher still, he now had to work to keep his hands off Emery, who looked sleekly delicious in a shiny white shirt, black slacks and another of her scarves, this one in jeweled holiday tones.

The woman was slowly shoving him straight over the edge.

They drove across the bridge that spanned the creek on the way to Raven's Nest, Carson McRaven's sprawling lodge. McRaven was a newcomer to Cold Creek Canyon and had purchased the ranch Nate had always known as the Wagon Wheel after the previous owner died in a ranch accident. Last summer, he had ended up marrying the widow who had sold him the land.

Nate had known Jenna Wheeler McRaven in high school. She had saved his bacon right after Suzi and John died by filling the freezer at the house with container after container of delicious food for them to eat in those first raw, terrible early days.

The McRavens' house was lit up, with a Christmas tree that had to be twice the size of the Hope Springs one blazing in the front window and lights framing just about every window.

He blinked a little at this exuberance. The few times Nate had met him, Carson McRaven didn't seem the sort to dive into the whole holiday spirit thing. But he supposed a man with four stepchildren probably had to make a few concessions.

The moment he parked the SUV and turned the vehicle ignition off, the girls climbed out and raced for the front door, leaving him to walk the short distance to the house alone with Emery.

He was intensely aware of her, her scent of cinnamon and vanilla and the roses the cold air put into her high cheekbones.

"How's Tallie today?" she asked just before they reached the steps into the house. "Did it take long for her to fall asleep again after the nightmare last night?"

He jerked his mind away from how badly he wanted to drag her against one of those porch supports and kiss her until they were both mindless.

"Okay," he answered. "A little quieter than normal, maybe. I really thought she was done with the nightmares. Right after the accident, she would wake up every night crying, but it's been several weeks since the last one."

"Poor thing. It makes your heart just break, doesn't it?"

"We all usually have a tough time going back to sleep afterward, but this one wasn't too bad. For the girls, anyway. I noticed your light was still on late."

She flashed him a quick look then turned her attention back to the step. "I was working on the quilts."

He had nearly forgotten them amid all that heated embrace and then all his angst over Tallie's nightmare. And, he was rather abashed to admit, over this stupid party he didn't want to attend.

"How are they coming?"

"Good," she answered, losing a little of the tension he'd noticed from the moment she slid into the SUV at the house. "I can't believe how fast they're coming together. Tallie's is nearly done and I should finish Claire's in plenty of time for you to put them under your tree tomorrow night."

Christmas Eve, he realized with a little spurt of shock. How could it possibly be here so soon?

Before he could answer, the door swung open and their host and hostess greeted them with friendly smiles.

"Nate!" Jenna wrapped him in a hug and kissed his cheek, reminding him anew why she had always been one of his favorite people at Pine Gulch High. "The girls rushed in a few moments ago so I figured you wouldn't be far behind. I'm so happy you made it."

He pulled away and introduced Emery, who was still hovering near the door. "Jenna, this is Emery Kendall. She's visiting the ranch from Virginia. Em, this is Jenna McRaven and her husband, Carson."

"Welcome!" Jenna exclaimed with another of her exuberant hugs while Carson shook Nate's hand.

"We're pretty casual tonight," Carson said. "The food is all set up buffet style in the dining room and most of the children are already in the pool. We've got adults stationed there to keep watch, don't worry."

"Thank you for inviting me," Emery said with a polite smile. "It's lovely to be included, even though I'm only visiting the area."

"We're happy to have you," Carson replied with a sincerity Nate hoped Emery didn't miss.

Before she could answer, though, Wade Dalton approached and held out his hand to Nate. Jenna, the proper hostess, began introducing Emery to him but Wade shook his head.

"We've met," Wade said with a smile. "Glad you decided to come after all."

Nate frowned. He'd always been struck by the resemblance between Wade and his father, but when he poured on the charm, the man was a dead ringer for Hank. He had a sudden insane urge to wrap his arm around Emery's shoulders and claim her as his for all the world to see.

Ridiculous. She wasn't his and she never would be.

That didn't stop him from having to swallow a growl when Wade gave her a broad smile.

"Carrie's going to be thrilled you're here. She's in the kitchen. I'll go let her know you and Nate are here."

She didn't answer, only nodded. But to Nate's shock, she didn't take her gaze off him as he walked away, following his progress away from them with a strange, intent expression.

Nate's stomach suddenly felt slick, greasy. He didn't want to see her sudden fascination with Wade Dalton. He wanted to pretend he had been completely mistaken about it.

Like father, like son, apparently.

Old Hank Dalton had never let a silly thing like his wedding ring interfere with his love life.

"Can I get you a drink?" Carson asked.

He shook his head, but Emery asked in a rather strangled voice for some ginger ale.

"Coming right up," he said, and headed for a table laden with drinks, just as Maggie Dalton walked past them with a tray of little shrimp skewers wrapped in bacon.

Though they looked delicious and he hadn't eaten any dinner, he didn't think he could choke down even one. He had completely lost his appetite.

"Hey, Sergeant," Maggie said with a smile. He gave her a smart salute, as he always did when he saw her, more out of respect than obligation since they were both retired, indoors and out of uniform.

If she hadn't left the military a few years earlier, Maggie would have outranked him, since she had been an army nurse lieutenant stationed in Afghanistan who had been badly injured when her clinic had been firebombed by terrorists. He had been in country at the time and had managed to visit her for a few moments before she had been shipped out to Germany for better medical care.

Given the extent of her injuries, he had been pretty sure she wouldn't make it, but Maggie was a fighter. Though she had lost her leg below the knee in the attack, she didn't let her injury stop her. Besides raising two toddlers, she worked as a nurse practitioner in her husband's medical clinic and volunteered in many community activities.

"How are things with the girls?" she asked him.

"Fine. We're managing."

She shook her head with a rueful laugh. "You Rangers are always so verbose."

Despite his distraction, he managed to smile. "It's all part of our charm."

Before she could answer, her husband, Jake, walked

into the room carrying one of their children, a little dark-haired boy with huge eyes and a wide, toothless smile.

"Hey, darlin'. Where's the diaper bag? This one stinks."

"Oh, I left it in the first bedroom off the kitchen when I changed Sofia. There's a changing table in there. Want me to take care of it?"

"No. I've got it," Jake said. "You can take the next one."

He kissed his wife on the cheek then turned to them. "Cavazos. Good to see you." He smiled at Emery. "Hi. I'm Jake Dalton. I don't think we've met."

Emery cleared her throat, a slightly dazed look in her eyes as she looked at the other man. "I'm Emery Kendall. I'm…staying at Hope Springs."

"Welcome to Pine Gulch. I'm sorry to run, but trust me, you don't want me hanging around with Mr. Stink-meister here."

When he walked away, Maggie turned to Emery. "You're the fabric designer from Virginia Caroline was talking about! I'm sorry I didn't make the connection. She was hoping you would come. Nate, I'm stealing your guest so she can come back to the kitchen and dish with us girls."

Before he could protest, Maggie slipped an arm through Emery's and tugged her away, leaving him temporarily on his own.

Since he didn't feel like standing around making more small talk, he headed toward the vast three-story atrium that housed the pool, as he suddenly realized he should have done the moment they arrived to make sure the girls were well-supervised.

The noise level was considerably larger in the pool atrium, with screams and shouts of glee amplified by the echoing space.

He found a few adults in the pool and several more standing in groups, talking while they kept watch over the fifteen or so energetic kids splashing around in the pool. Seth Dalton was one of them. Though he was fully dressed and stood on the side of the pool, he was tossing a wet beach ball back and forth to several of the kids. He didn't seem to mind being splashed every time the ball came his way.

Nate supposed he should be grateful Emery wasn't around to fall for the youngest Dalton brother, too, since he was the one with the reputation of a heartbreaker, before he'd settled down and married the elementary school principal, anyway.

"Uncle Nate! Uncle Nate!" Tallie's yell from the diving board added to the din in the room. "Watch me. I'm gonna jump."

"Okay. I'm watching," he called back and had to smile as she did a perfect cannonball into the water before resurfacing and paddling to the side.

"Did you see me?" she called out when she reached the side.

"I did. You were awesome."

"I'm gonna do it again. Keep watching."

He smiled again. "You got it, kid."

He watched her jump two more times before she grew bored and started tossing the beach ball with the other kids.

"This has to be a big adjustment for you."

He looked away from the pool to find Seth had joined him. Though he wasn't very inclined to think favorably of any of the Daltons right now, he knew his jealousy was unjustified and unfair. The man was trying to make conversation and wasn't that the whole point of a gathering like this?

"It's not exactly where I expected to find myself, four months ago," he admitted. "But we're settling in."

"I can't say I know what you're going through. It must

be tough to step in after all the pain those girls have been through. But I do know a little about suddenly becoming part of a ready-made family."

Jenny Boyer Dalton had two children from a previous marriage, Nate remembered. "How long did it take before you stopped feeling like you were completely out of your depth?"

"I'm waiting for that feeling to hit me any day now." Seth grinned. "But then, it's only been three years. I take comfort from Wade, who's been a father since Natalie was born eleven years ago. He has four kids now and still doesn't know what he's doing."

"That's why I was smart enough to marry a woman who's brilliant at the whole thing," another voice interjected and Nate looked over to find Wade had joined them.

Some covert ops specialist he was. He hadn't heard the man's approach over the noise from the pool. For one wild second, he wanted to shove the bastard into the water, but he knew that was unfair. Probably.

"We're comparing notes on being thrown into the deep end when it comes to kids," Seth said.

"My only advice is, just try to keep your head above water and paddle like hell. Not much else you can do," Wade said.

Despite his—okay, he could admit it—jealousy, Nate had to smile. "My arms are just about ready to fall off," he admitted.

"You've got it tough because you're on your own," Seth said. "Wade did that for a few years after his first wife died."

"It wasn't easy on anybody," Wade agreed. "At least I had my mom to help out. I don't know what we would have done without her."

His voice trailed off and he looked embarrassed for a

moment, as if he'd suddenly remembered what had happened between Nate's mother and Hank Dalton and why Linda Cavazos wasn't in the picture.

"Caroline tells me you're thinking about closing the guest ranch," he said after an awkward moment.

"Thinking about it. I haven't made a decision yet, but as I've been going over the ranch accounts and familiarizing myself with the books, I'm figuring out it's a small part of our revenue base, but ends up taking a disproportionate expenditure of energy and resources. Besides that, I'm not sure I'm cut out for the hospitality industry."

"You planning to expand the ranching side of things, then?"

Why is it any of your damn business? he wanted to ask, but he wouldn't be outright rude. "I haven't decided anything yet."

"I'm asking because I might have a lead on some summer grazing allotments that are coming up for bid, if you're interested."

He blinked, stunned by the offer. Grazing allotments from the federal government that allowed ranchers to move their cattle onto forest service land for the summer were highly coveted, more valuable around here than gold. "Why don't you want them?"

Wade shrugged. "We've used the same allotments for thirty years and they meet our current needs just fine." He paused. "I will add, though, that if you think you might end up selling Hope Springs altogether, I'd like first crack at it."

He stared at the other man as all his old feelings of resentment and suspicion welled up in his chest.

"I'm still weighing my options," he said firmly, when what he wanted to say was that he would sell the ranch to the Daltons the minute palm trees started growing at Hope Springs in January.

"Fair enough," Wade said. He didn't seem at all offended. "I just wanted you to know."

After Christmas he was going to have to make a decision. He couldn't continue waffling. Either he had to give a hundred percent to the ranch or he ought to sell it and take the girls somewhere else. Maybe not sell it to the Daltons, but to someone.

He didn't know what he would do besides being a soldier or a rancher, but he could figure something out.

If he didn't keep paddling, the only other option was to sink like a stone, and he wasn't ready to do that yet.

She didn't belong here.

The food was delicious, the conversation interesting, the company warm and friendly toward her. As she sat in the kitchen surrounded by women talking about their children and the holidays and memories they shared, Emery couldn't escape the inevitable conclusion that she was once more on the outside looking in.

She took a small bite of a cranberry tart. On some subconscious level she registered it was delicious, with just the perfect combination of sweetness and edge. But she was barely aware of what she ate.

Part of her longed, quite fiercely, to be part of their close-knit group. She wanted to be teased by Seth Dalton, to have the right to shower gifts on her nieces and nephews, to have these women as her friends and sisters.

This craving for a big, noisy, crazy family was as fierce as it was unexpected. Maybe it was because her mother had been her last remaining relative and her death left Emery unutterably alone. Or maybe that longing had always lurked somewhere inside her, buried deep by the reality of being an only child of only children.

Or not.

She swallowed the last morsel of the tart. For all she knew, maybe Hank Dalton had a dozen brothers, and she had a fleet of cousins she knew nothing about.

How would the Dalton brothers and their families react if they knew the outsider from Virginia shared half their DNA?

One brief sentence. That's all it would take. She could tell Caroline or Jenny Dalton right now and the word would spread in a moment.

What would they think if they knew she was Hank Dalton's daughter with a tourist who had indulged in a brief affair twenty-seven years ago?

She sighed. The idea of spilling the news to them all seemed selfish and desperate suddenly. How could it be anything else? She was the one with everything to gain by sharing the information. She would have an instant extended family. Noisy children and darling chubby babies and three instant sisters-in-law to love.

What would they all have to gain? Only her. A boring textile designer who had spent her entire life trying—and failing—to be perfect.

She was quite certain telling the Daltons about her blood link to them would have unexpected ripples of consequence, like the ripples from a rock thrown into a pond.

"Emery, do you mind taking that plate of spinach pinwheels out to the great room?" Jenna McRaven asked. Her hostess was warm and friendly and, true to the girls' assurances, cooked like a dream.

"Oh, and don't let my husband near them or no one else

will get any," Jenna said with a grin. "You can tell Carson if he puts up any kind of a fuss that I'm saving a private stash for him for later."

Emery managed to return her smile then walked into the great room where most of the guests had gathered. Several new people had arrived while she was in the kitchen. As she was setting the spinach rolls on the overflowing buffet table, an older woman in a glittery silver lamé blouse snatched one up.

"I love these things," she said with an expression of glee. "I was hoping Jenna would make them."

"They are good," Emery said politely.

"I don't think I know you," the woman said, squinting at her. "Are you a friend of the McRavens?"

"I'm actually a guest at Hope Springs until the end of the week. I'm here with Nate Cavazos."

The older woman's features lit up into a particularly lovely smile. "You must be the woman from Virginia. Caroline and Wade told me you might be coming. I'm Marjorie Montgomery. Used to be Dalton. Wade's mother."

If she hadn't already set the platter of food down, Emery was certain she would have dumped the whole thing all over Marjorie Dalton Montgomery's feet in her shock.

This was the wife Hank Dalton had neglected to mention to Emery's mother while he was busy seducing the starry-eyed girl fascinated by the romance of the West. The little she had eaten all night seemed to churn greasily in her stomach. Hank Dalton's wife. How foolish of her not to have even a moment of consideration for the woman in all this.

"How are you enjoying your stay?" Marjorie asked.

"It's been lovely," she managed to say through her suddenly dry mouth. "Everyone has been more than kind."

"Folks around here take care of each other, whether you've lived here all your life or just dropped in for a visit," she said with a warm smile. "Why, take my second husband. Four years ago, he moved here without knowing a soul but me. And Caroline, of course. She's his daughter. Which makes her my stepdaughter and my daughter-in-law both. Anyway, four years later, now Quinn has his own real estate office and he's on the Pine Gulch town council. Everybody warmed to him real quick."

"I've found everyone around here very friendly," Emery said.

"Carrie tells me you're a textile designer."

"That's right. I design fabric, mostly for the home. Pillows, curtains, that sort of thing."

"Fabric stores are my favorite places to shop!" Marjorie exclaimed. "I belong to a quilting group in town. It's one of my passions. We get together every other Thursday and do about eight or nine quilts a year, then we auction them off for charity every year."

"I'm making a couple of quilts right now, actually," Emery said. "I could have used your help today when I was piecing them."

They talked a few more moments about quilts, until a petite Hispanic woman who reminded Emery of Maggie Dalton approached them. After a few moments, their conversation shifted to a recent library board meeting.

As she listened to their conversation with half an ear about people she didn't know and future events she wouldn't be part of, the grim truth settled over her, dank and overpowering.

She couldn't tell the Daltons her identity. Not when doing so would force ugly secrets up like sludge from the ground. If she shared with them the story her mother had told her, she would have to tell Marjorie Dalton Montgomery that her husband had cheated on her when she had three young boys, the youngest probably only in kindergarten.

As much as she would love a ready-made family, the chance to have a genuine place among them, how could she justify the hurt she would likely cause along the way?

Her chest ached at what she would be giving up, but she knew it was the right decision.

She should never have come to Pine Gulch. Better never to have met the Daltons and find them people she was almost certain she could like and admire than to have to carry that knowledge with her when she left.

But if she had never come here, she wouldn't have met Nate and the girls.

As if her thoughts had summoned him, she heard Nate's deep voice and then Tallie's higher-pitched one. She turned to find them in a corner of the room. His niece must have decided she was tired of swimming. She had dressed again and Nate was busy toweling off her dark hair with a beach towel decorated with the Little Mermaid.

Something fluttered through her chest as she watched the tough, dangerous soldier take care of the little girl.

Leaving them would be extraordinarily difficult. All three of them—Nate, Tallie and Claire—had somehow sneaked into her heart when she wasn't looking.

She would have to, though. And she would survive. She had endured the loss of her child and her marriage and her parents. She could endure few more losses.

At least she hoped so.

Chapter Twelve

Christmas Eve was her least favorite day of the year.

After the alarm on her cell phone buzzed her awake just before sunrise, Emery lay in bed and gazed at the log beams of her rented cabin, wishing she had more of a stomach for drinking so she could spend the day in an alcohol-induced stupor.

Her arms never felt as empty as they did on this day, little Gracie's birthday and date of her death.

If her world hadn't changed so painfully and abruptly two years ago today, her baby girl would have been toddling around their house in Hampton, pulling ornaments off the tree, gabbing away little nonsense words.

She would have been a good mother. Her experience the past few days with the girls verified that for her. She would have adored showing Gracie the magic and wonder of life in general and Christmas in particular.

She sat up and used the corner of the flannel sheet to dab at her eyes. She had far too much work to do to indulge in sitting here feeling sorry for herself, swallowed by her grief, and she was suddenly enormously grateful for that.

Though she had worked late in the night after the party at the McRavens' to finish Claire's quilt, she still needed to bind it and then finish machine-quilting Tallie's. She was going to have to sew her fingers to the bone in order to get them both done in time.

The reminder energized her, renewed her, and she slid from the bed. The best cure for self-pity and sadness was to pour all those negative energies into doing something positive for someone else.

Sewing those quilts for the girls was better for her psyche than months of therapy.

Several hours later, she sewed the last seam on the binding of Claire's quilt, then eased her chair away from the sewing machine, suddenly conscious that every muscle in her body ached, from her tense shoulders to her dry eyelids to the arch of her foot from pressing the sewing machine pedal.

She needed a long soak in a hot tub.

Or at least a nap.

She glanced at her watch and was stunned to see it was after four. She had been sewing virtually nonstop for ten hours. No wonder she felt as if she'd been trampled in a cattle stampede.

She picked up the quilt and carried it into her bedroom, where she had spread Tallie's quilt earlier in order to admire the finished product.

Though she had used the same mix of fabrics pieced from their parents' clothing in both of them, she had opted for different designs to show their individual personalities. Tallie's was whimsical and cute, a trail of colorful butterflies dancing across the pale pink background, offset by the brown edge. Claire's was a little more grown-up, a traditional Lone Star pattern with a large six-pointed star in the center, radiating color out to the edge.

She had used a mix of materials snipped from Suzi's and John's clothing in complementary colors and she had chosen brown backing for Tallie's and pink for Claire's. Considering the short time she had to work on them, she was amazed at how they'd turned out. She only hoped the girls would like them.

Her stomach grumbled and she frowned when she realized she hadn't eaten since the quick egg-white omelet she'd made for protein that morning.

She was standing at the refrigerator poring over her limited options for Christmas Eve dinner and had just about settled on a grilled cheese sandwich when she suddenly heard what sounded like muffled crying, followed quickly by a knock on her front door.

The girls!

"Coming. Just a moment," she called out, then rushed to the bedroom where the quilts were still spread and yanked closed the door, grateful she had already gathered all the scraps from the clothing she had cut up and tucked them carefully away in the boxes Nate had left on her doorstep.

Her tight shoulder muscles yelped in protest when she reached to open the door, but she forgot all about her aches and her worry that they would discover the quilts prematurely when she saw the two distressed little faces on the other side.

"What is it? Are you hurt? Is it your uncle?"

"Everything's ruined!" The cry was all the more distressing coming from Claire. Solid, dependable, serious Claire.

"What's ruined, honey? Come inside out of the cold and tell me what's wrong."

Both girls hurried into the room in tears, though at first glance it appeared to Emery that Tallie was crying more in sympathy with her sister than out of any real upset.

"We messed up everything," Tallie sniffled.

"I tried so hard," Claire said. "We wanted everything to be perfect for Uncle Nate but the *masa* is lumpy and gross and won't spread on the cornhusks and I burned my finger on the chili peppers and now the stupid tamales won't roll right."

She blinked, more than a little lost. "You're making tamales?"

Claire nodded. "We always have tamales on Christmas Eve. Our mama used to tell us *she* always had tamales on Christmas Eve so we thought Uncle Nate would like them. Joanie helped us buy the stuff before she ran off and I've been hiding it in so Uncle Nate wouldn't know. Only I can't make them right and now everything is *ruined.*"

Her tears seemed disproportionate to the current crisis and Emery pulled her close, her heart aching as she realized Claire's distress likely had more to do with missing her mother than out of any tamale-induced trauma.

"We thought maybe you could help us," Tallie said. "You can fix everything."

"Me?" She hoped her gulp wasn't audible to the girls. "I'm afraid I don't know anything about tamales."

"We have Mama's recipe book," Claire said. "I know what we're supposed to do, I just can't seem to do it."

She was exhausted, her muscles tight and achy, and

cooking wasn't her area of expertise in the first place. But how could she simply ignore their suffering?

"Where's your uncle?"

"Doing chores," Claire answered. "He was supposed to be back already, but he called and said he had a problem with one of the horses and he'd be up as soon as he could. Dinner's never going to be done because tamales have to cook *forever* and we only rolled four of them."

"Will you help us?" Tallie begged.

"Oh, please." Claire added her voice. "Christmas Eve will be completely ruined if you don't."

They sounded so dramatic that she would have smiled if they hadn't both been perfectly in earnest.

This wasn't about tamales, she thought again. This was about two grieving little girls trying to hang on to traditions that had been lost with their parents. She didn't have the heart to refuse, even though she didn't think she would be any more proficient at the task than they seemed to be.

"Of course I'll help you." She ignored the twinge in her muscles when she reached for her coat and scarf. After she had put them on, she reached a hand out to each girl.

"Let's go. Christmas Eve tamales coming right up."

The girls were going to skin him.

He was late and they were going to be starving by the time he managed to heat up the lasagna from the freezer he had planned for dinner. He should have called again and had Claire put it in, but he'd gotten distracted in the barn and it had completely slipped his mind.

So dinner would be late. No big deal, he assured himself. Maybe if the girls stayed up later, they might have an easier time getting to sleep on Christmas Eve. Of course, they probably wouldn't be happy about having to wait for their dinner, but he hoped he could make it up to them when he explained the reason for the delay.

He pushed open the door. "Hey, girls," he called, "I have a surprise for you."

And then the scents washed over him, wave after wave, and he froze.

Suddenly he was a kid again, spending Christmas Eve surrounded by the delectable scents of corn flour and peppers and pork roast, in an endless agony of anticipation as he waited for their traditional tamales to steam.

What in the hell?

He followed his nose to the kitchen and had his second shock in as many minutes when he found Emery Kendall working at the kitchen island, wearing a splattered apron and looking decidedly bedraggled, her sleek blond hair falling out of its knot.

"Whoa. What's going on in here?"

"Tamales!" Tallie exclaimed, her little features flush with excitement. "We're making tamales, Uncle Nate. Can you smell them?"

"We always had tamales on Christmas Eve," Claire added, a little defiantly. "Mama said *she* always had them when you were kids and you did, too."

"We messed them up the first time and we were *so* upset," Tallie confided. "We thought Christmas was ruined for *sure* and then I said maybe Emery could help us fix them and Claire said that was a good idea and so we went and asked her and she said okay and this batch is just perfect."

"I wouldn't say perfect," Emery muttered. "But I hope they're edible."

He met her gaze and she looked frazzled and slightly

helpless and completely beautiful, with her cheeks pink from the steam coming from the stove.

"Wow. I haven't had real homemade tamales in years."

He had a sudden vivid memory of this very kitchen, when he was probably a few years younger than Tallie, during the time he still considered the good years before his father died.

His mother would spend several days before Christmas making tamales from the recipe she learned from his *abuela*. They would have a big party with relatives and friends from all over southern Idaho. Cousins, uncles, aunts. It had been crazy and noisy and wonderful.

He tended to dwell on all the ugliness that came after with his mother and forget there had been plenty of good times along the way, before everything went wrong.

"They smell *delicioso*."

The girls both giggled and he smiled at them. His gaze shifted again to Emery's and something sparked between them, something sweet and bright.

"You are a woman of many talents," he murmured. "How does a blue blood Virginia textile designer know how to make tamales?"

She made a face. "I don't, as I'm sure you'll figure out when they're finally done. I followed your sister's recipe as best I could and then ended up making a frantic call to my friend Freddie—short for Frederica—and she walked me through it."

He peered into the steamer at two dozen pale rolled cornhusks and his stomach rumbled. "They look perfect. I just might have to eat them all."

"No!" Tallie exclaimed. "We get some, too. We're the ones who made them!"

"We'll have to see who's the quickest." He winked at her and found Emery gazing at him with an expression in her blue eyes he couldn't identify.

He wanted to bask in it suddenly, to burn this memory into his mind along with all those years of Christmas parties.

"How soon before they'll be done?"

"We actually had enough for two batches so you'll have some to freeze later. We're ready to put the second batch in now and the first batch will be done in about a half hour."

"Perfect. That will give me time to clean the barn off me." The words suddenly reminded him of the past two hours' effort. "Oh! I nearly forgot. I came in to tell you I've got a Christmas Eve surprise for you."

"What is it?" Tallie exclaimed. "Is it a present? Can we open it?"

"I guess you could say it's a present that's already been opened. Actually, it's not my surprise at all. It's Annabelle's. She had her foal three weeks early. That's what took me so long."

Why did girls always have to use that high-pitched squeal when they were excited? No "yeah, dudes" or fist-pounding around here. They just pierced his eardrums with their glee then hugged each other and danced around the kitchen.

"We have to go see it! Right now!" Claire exclaimed.

"After dinner, okay?" he said. "Otherwise the tamales will steam too long and they'll be ruined. You've put so much work into them, I want to do dinner justice."

They didn't look thrilled at the delay, but they didn't argue. "Uncle Nate, Emery can stay and have dinner with us tonight, can't she?" Tallie asked.

He shot a look at Emery at the stove just in time to see

her mouth open a little in surprise at the backhanded invitation. Her surprise quickly shifted to discomfort.

"It's Christmas Eve, honey," she answered. "It's a time for families and I'm not really part of your family."

"But if you hadn't helped us with the tamales, we would have starved!"

She smiled a little at this dramatic wail, but he thought he saw sadness in her eyes. He wondered at it for a moment then suddenly remembered. This was Christmas Eve, the two-year anniversary of her baby's death. His chest felt tight, achy.

"I'm sure your uncle wouldn't have let you starve. He would have found something for you to eat."

"I had a lasagna in the freezer just waiting to be warmed up. But traditional tamales will be much, much better." He paused, wishing he could take her hand in front of the girls. "We'd love to have you join us. Will you stay?"

He waited for her answer, startled by how very much he wanted her to say yes.

"I'm starving," she admitted. "I didn't have lunch. And since the tamales won't be done for some time, I'd love to walk back to the cabin for a moment to clean up."

He wanted to tell her she looked beautiful, that seeing her with all her perfection a little bit messed up only seemed to add to her appeal. Instead, he only smiled.

"Meet you back here in half an hour, then."

Dinner was an unqualified success.

The tamales were fantastic, rich and spicy and very much like the recipe he remembered from his childhood.

Afterward, they laughed and joked while they cleaned up together and then bundled up to walk down to the barn to see Annabelle's yuletide present, all spindly legs and big eyes and baffled expression.

"Oh! He's beautiful!" Tallie exclaimed while Claire folded her hands together and tucked them against her heart.

"He's a she," Nate said, completely enjoying their delight. "I figured you two could pick out a name for her."

"What about Holly?" Claire asked.

"Or Chrissy?" Tallie said. "For Christmas."

"What about Noël?" Emery joined into their name game.

"Noël! I *love* it!" Claire said.

"Me, too," her sister declared.

"Noël it is, then. That work okay for you, Annabelle?"

The mare blew her lips out in a raspberry that sounded very much like agreement and all of them laughed.

The girls continued to be entranced with the foal, but after a moment he saw Emery ease slightly away from them to lean against the railing of the opposite stall. Even though he knew in his gut the smartest move would be to keep as much distance as possible, he couldn't seem to resist joining her.

"I finished the quilts this afternoon," she said in an undertone so the girls couldn't hear. "Actually, I had just sewn the last stitch about ten minutes before the girls rushed down to the cabin in the midst of the great tamale catastrophe."

"You did?"

"Yes. And even though this probably sounds terribly vain, I have to admit, they turned out beautifully. I think they'll love them."

"I'm sure they will."

"When I went back to the cabin to change before dinner, I wrapped them both up for you. If you want, you can pick them up when you transfer all the presents from the other cabin."

Oh, right. He still had to drag everything up to the house and put it under the tree later. In light of the fact that she had just spent two days sewing quilts for the girls, he had little to complain about, even if the prospect of filling stockings and making everything just right did feel a little overwhelming right about now.

"I have a better idea," he said suddenly. "We talked about giving them the nightgowns tonight, but let's give them the quilts instead. Then they can sleep wrapped in them and maybe it will feel a little like their parents are with them on Christmas Eve."

Her smile was soft and radiant, like sunshine creeping over the mountaintops on a frigid January day, and he wanted to stay here in this cold barn and bask in it.

"What a wonderful idea!"

No. He didn't want to bask in her smile. He wanted to capture it with his own mouth and absorb it inside him. Somehow that made it all worse.

"Let's do it now. We can pick them up at your cabin and then go back to the house for the girls to open them."

"I don't need to be there with you," she protested. "It's a family time."

He stopped her argument by taking her hands in his and squeezing her fingers, even though he knew touching her probably wasn't the greatest idea. "You absolutely *do* need to be there. I know you must have worked incredibly hard to finish them on such short notice. I want you there when the girls see them."

She shot a quick look at Tallie and Claire, still busy laughing at the foal's ungainly steps. "Are you sure? I don't want to overstep."

"You deserve to be there for the big unveiling." He

paused, compelled to be truthful. "And without you, I'm afraid none of us would be having much of a Christmas. You made it all happen, Em. From the Christmas tree to the tamales. It was all you."

In the dim light inside the barn, he could see color rise on her high cheekbones.

"I'd love to be there when they open the quilts," she murmured. "If you're sure I'm not intruding."

He should say yes. He should tell her she had been intruding into his mind since the moment she showed up at the ranch with her deep blue eyes and her rented SUV full of suitcases.

But he only shook his head. "It's going to be great. Let's do it."

"Please tell us!" Claire begged for the twentieth time as they left Emery's cabin and headed back to the main house a short time later. "What's in the boxes?"

"You'll find out soon enough," Nate said with a grin. "You can open them after you change into your pajamas."

"But I can't wait that long," Tallie exclaimed. "I know I can't. The suspense is *killing* me," she added.

"I hope not," her uncle answered. "Because then the surprise Emery has for you will just have to go to some other eight-year-old with brown pigtails."

"Stop teasing me, Uncle Nate. You don't know any other eight-year-olds with brown pigtails."

"I'll just have to find one," he said pitilessly when they reached the door.

She glared at him, though she looked more excited than upset. "You will not. But okay. I'll go change into my pajamas. Do we have to take showers?"

"It wouldn't hurt," Emery said before Nate could answer. "We all got a little messy while we were making tamales and who knows what you might have picked up in the horse barn? But I bet you two can take the fastest showers on record."

"Me first!" Tallie exclaimed and she headed up the stairs. Claire rolled her eyes at her sister. She followed at a more sedate pace, but after three steps, she started taking them two at a time.

Too late, Emery realized the girls' defection left her alone with Nate, something she really hadn't been since that heated embrace on the sofa of the other guest cabin. "I'll just set this under the tree," she said after an awkward pause.

He followed her into the great room and she was painfully aware of him. They both set the large boxes next to the Christmas tree, then to her secret relief, Nate moved to the fireplace to stir the coals and add another log.

While he was distracted, Emery enjoyed the holiday scene, from the Christmas tree to the new stockings she had made for Nate and the girls, which now hung proudly from the mantel.

It was a wonderful room, with its soaring vaulted ceilings, log walls and the unpretentious decor. This was exactly the mood she wanted to capture in the textiles for the Spencer Hotels property in Livingston, this completely natural sense of the American West. Warm, homey, completely right, here amid the beauty of their surroundings.

Nerves fluttered through her like sparks shooting up the chimney when Nate finished at the fireplace and joined her on the sofa. She was again aware of him, the spicy, masculine scent that clung to his skin, the tiny hint of an evening shadow.

"I'm more excited than they are for them to open the presents," he confessed, "and I haven't even seen the quilts."

She smiled, doing her best to ignore her reaction to him. "Well, I've seen more than enough of them and I'm still over the moon. I just hope they like them."

"They'll love them. It's a wonderful thing you've done."

His dark eyes lit up with warmth and something else and she couldn't seem to look away.

"Emery—" he began, but whatever he intended to say was lost when they heard footsteps rocketing down the stairs. Those girls instinctively knew when to make an entrance, she thought wryly.

"I win! I win!" Tallie exclaimed and she raced into the room in a navy blue plaid nightgown.

"Not by much," Claire retorted as she skidded to a stop beside her sister. She wore waffle-weave long john pajamas with Tweety Bird on the front.

"Is it time?" Tallie asked. "Can we open them now?"

Nate slanted a look to Emery that she couldn't quite read, then he looked back at his nieces and cleared his throat. "In a minute. Sit down first."

The girls sat on the opposite sofa, though Tallie looked poised to start bouncing off the walls any moment now.

"I owe you girls an apology."

"Why?" Claire asked.

"Well, I should have asked you before about the Christmas Eve traditions you used to do with your mom and dad. I should have known about the tamales. Is there anything else we haven't done today that you used to do with your mom and dad?"

The girls looked puzzled for a moment, their brows furrowed, and then Claire spoke quietly. "Well, every year

Dad used to read us the Christmas story before we went to bed. Not the ''Twas The Night Before Christmas' one. The one in the Bible.''

Nate looked a little taken aback as if he hadn't quite been expecting that answer, but he quickly recovered. "Sure. We can do that, if you know where I can find a Bible."

"I know," Tallie said. She moved to the bookshelf in the corner and after a moment of searching through the spines, she pulled down a white leather book with gilt edges.

"It was our mama's," Claire said, her voice low.

Emotions swelled in Emery's throat as Tallie clutched the book to her chest for a moment then finally handed it over to Nate, who had moved to the plump easy chair.

Nate held it for a long moment, his thumb tracing his sister's gold embossed name on the front. He made no move to open it.

"Luke, Chapter 2," she said, trying to be helpful.

His looked up, his mouth quirked into a half smile. "I might not be a particularly religious man, but I do know that much. Thanks, though."

He opened the Bible, leafed through the pages and finally found the right book and chapter. Much to her surprise, as soon as he started to read, both girls joined her on the larger sofa, Tallie snuggling against Emery's shoulder until she put her arm around her and pulled the girl close.

Oh, she was going to have a terrible time leaving this place. The lump in her throat expanded. She felt enfolded in the warm, accepting love of these girls and knew it would break her heart into a million tiny, jagged shards to leave them. Next Christmas and every other Christmas would be painful and empty when she compared them to this one that she had started out dreading so much.

She wouldn't think about that now. Why waste this perfect moment by borrowing tomorrow's pain?

Nate finished reading, his voice solemn as he read the last words. When he closed the book, they sat in silence for a long moment and then he looked up.

He seemed surprised to find them all snuggled together and his eyes glittered with a sudden intensity.

"That was nice," Tallie said solemnly. "It gives me a really happy feeling inside."

"Me, too," Emery said in perfect accord.

"I think this is the perfect moment to open your presents," he said, his voice barely above a whisper in keeping with the hushed reverence in the house.

The girls brightened with excitement, but they didn't rip into the presents in a mad rush, as Emery might have expected. Instead, they knelt carefully on the rug by the tree and began to gently peel away the wrapping paper.

Tallie finished first and Emery held her breath as the girl folded over the flaps on the cardboard box. She reached inside and pulled out the quilt, her pixie features twisted with confusion.

"It's a blanket."

"It's a quilt," Emery explained.

She unfolded it, her eyes wide. "It's pretty," she said, then looked at her sister. "You got one, too!"

Claire pulled hers out, her hands gentle, almost reverent, as she spread it across the rug.

"I love the star!"

"Mine has butterflies," Tallie said. "Can you see them, Uncle Nate?"

"I see them. Does any of the fabric look familiar?" Nate prompted.

Claire picked it up and traced the most prominent fabric of the star pattern, lavender with tiny, pale pink flowers. "Mama used to have a skirt like this." She gasped. "And this one looks like Dad's favorite pajama bottoms."

"Emery used material from the boxes of your mom's and dad's clothing to make the quilt."

The girls looked stunned. "You did?" Claire gasped.

"I thought maybe when you had your quilts wrapped around you, it might feel a little bit like you were getting big hugs from your mom and dad."

Claire's eyes softened and she immediately wrapped her quilt around her shoulders. "You're right. That's just what it feels like," she whispered, looking thrilled.

Tallie did the same, but suddenly her eyes filled with tears and she let out a ragged little whimper that turned into another and another until she was sobbing.

Nate went to her and pulled her onto his lap, quilt and all. "You don't have to use it if it's going to make you upset," he said, sounding somewhat panicked by her tears. "I'll put it away. Maybe in a few years you'll want it."

"Oh, sweetheart, I'm so sorry," Emery added, feeling wretched. "I thought it would make you happy."

"No!" Tallie burst out when Nate reached to take the quilt from her. She held on to it tightly, even as her shoulders trembled. "I didn't mean to cry," she wailed. "I'm sorry. But please don't take it. These are sad tears *and* happy tears. I really want to put it on my bed. If I sleep with it, I know I won't have any more nightmares."

"Oh, sweetheart." Nate held her close, his chin resting on her glossy dark hair.

Her heartbreaking sobs subsided after a moment and she wiped her eyes on Nate's shirt, but he didn't seem to mind.

"Can you read us something else, Uncle Nate?" Tallie asked.

"Like what?"

"Mom's favorite Christmas story was *The Polar Express*," Claire said. "Maybe that one."

Nate seemed relieved to have something concrete to do besides holding a distressed little girl. "All right. One more story and then bed, okay?"

The girls agreed. This time, both of them sat snuggled in their quilts beside him, leaving Emery alone. That was as it should be, she thought. They were creating their own traditions, making their own version of family.

"All right," he said when he finished the last page. "Now time for bed. Santa can't show up until you're both asleep."

Since the girls had been emphatic more than once to her that they knew the whole Santa story, Emery was surprised at their ready compliance. She supposed there was something about Christmas Eve that allowed even doubters to put aside their skepticism for one night and believe in a little magic.

"I'm super sleepy," Tallie claimed.

"Me, too," Claire said, stifling a yawn that certainly looked genuine.

"Up you go," Nate said. "I'll come tuck you in."

"Can Emery come, too?"

He sent a swift look in her direction and she saw uncertainty flash there. She was about to let him off the hook by telling the girls she needed to sleep and should be heading back to her cabin, but Nate surprised her by nodding.

"Sure," he said. "If she doesn't mind."

"I don't mind," she said.

She helped Claire gather her quilt and carry the trailing ends up the stairs while Nate did the same for Tallie.

A few moments later, both girls were settled in their beds, their comforters replaced by the brand-new quilts that seemed somehow to fit perfectly in their bedrooms, as if they had always been there.

Emery kissed Tallie's cheek, touched to see the girl's fingers tracing the different textured fabric of the butter-flies dancing across the quilt. Ridged corduroy from a pair of her father's slacks, denim from a work shirt, a deep purple satin poly blend from one of Suzi's blouses.

All the hours of work and the aching muscles were a distant memory, lost in the joy of seeing both girls find comfort in her creations.

"Sleep well, sweetheart," Emery said.

"Merry Christmas, Emery." She was quiet for a moment, then smiled sleepily. "It's a night for angels, isn't it?"

Tears burned behind her eyes, but Emery smiled. "I think so, sweetheart. Sweet dreams."

Part of her had that same wild wish that she had never come to Hope Springs, never had the chance to fall in love with these grieving girls. But she couldn't regret it when they had taught her so many lessons.

When she and Nate returned downstairs, he seemed a little distant and distracted. Probably wishing she would just go home and leave him alone, she thought. She opened her mouth to tell him she needed to do just that but he surprised her once more.

"I have no right to ask you any more favors since you've already done so much," he began.

"But?"

He sighed. "But I could use help with one more thing, if I haven't presumed entirely too much."

"How can I help?"

"I've never done the whole Christmas Eve thing. Putting out the stockings and the presents under the tree and everything. I'm pretty sure I'll screw it up on my own and leave everything a big jumbled mess."

She found his request almost unbearably sweet. "Of course. Although since I…don't have children, I'm not the world's biggest expert in that particular arena, either."

"But you know what looks good. You did such a great job decorating the house and then wrapping everything so nicely, I hate to just throw all the gifts under the tree. The only problem is, we're going to have to wait a few moments until they're asleep."

"Why don't I stay here with the girls while they fall asleep and you can go down to the cabin for the gifts? By the time you bring them all back, the girls should be asleep."

"Brilliant idea." He smiled a little. "See how much I needed your help?"

He tossed another log on the fire while Emery sank onto the sofa gratefully as her stiff muscles reminded her of the day's exertions.

When she heard him leave a moment later, she leaned back against the sofa cushion, watching the Christmas tree lights twinkle against the dark window and sorting through the emotions of the evening.

She had been dreading Christmas so much this year, the first holiday without her mother, the anniversary of Gracie's death.

How could she ever have guessed this would turn out to be the most perfect ever? From sewing the quilts to making cookies with the girls to decorating the house. She had loved all of it.

She closed her eyes, but the lights still seemed to glisten behind her eyelids. She would only rest for a moment, she told herself as exhaustion crept over her.

Just until he returned…

Chapter Thirteen

Nate carefully loaded the last box of gifts into the cargo space of the SUV, closed the hatch, then paused for a moment to gaze up at the night. This Christmas Eve was a cold one, with no cloud cover to hold in any warmth. The night was clear and beautiful, with a vast glitter of stars overhead.

He couldn't help thinking about his past few Christmas Eves in the desert. Two years ago his team had been in southern Iraq and last year he'd been in the frigid mountains of Afghanistan.

This one was much better than any in recent memory, he was forced to admit. Between the tamales and the miracle of the tiny foal and that very tender moment when the girls opened their quilts, he felt more connected to life and the future than he had in a long, long time.

For the first time since he came back to Idaho, he was feeling good about what might come next. A year from now, he would be much more prepared for the holidays and everything the girls might expect from them.

The only problem was, this year was going to be a hard act to follow, especially without Emery.

The thought of her leaving seemed to take a lot of luster from the stars overhead. He pushed it away, just as he used to make himself ignore the frustrations and fears of the battlefield so he could focus on what needed to be done.

There would be time to miss Emery later. Right now, he needed to take care of business, which meant hauling the girls' Christmas booty up to the house.

When he drove back to the house, he let himself in the front door quietly, with a careful look up the stairs to make sure the girls weren't peeking down from the landing.

"So do you think the coast is clear yet?" Nate whispered as he entered the great room.

When no one answered, he was grimly aware of a sharp clutch of panic. But reason intruded. She couldn't have left already, not when he had asked for her help. That wasn't in her nature. His gaze swept the room and he exhaled with relief when he saw her stretched out on the same sofa she had slept on the night of the storm. She lay on her side, her blond hair drifting over her shoulders and her folded hands tucked under her cheek like a child's.

She was serenely lovely in sleep, her darker lashes fanning her cheekbones and those classical features relaxed. He wanted to push away a strand of hair from her cheek, but decided not to wake her.

How late into the night had she worked to finish the quilts for the girls? When he thought of her hunched over a sewing machine, pouring such care and compassion into the work for two girls she barely knew, he could hardly breathe around the ache in his chest.

Something soft and tender swelled inside him as he watched her sleep and for one crazy moment, he wanted to jerk her off the couch and send her away.

That panic returned a thousandfold, especially when he realized he would rather take on a hundred enemy fighters on his own from a vulnerable position in a box canyon than have to face these fragile, terrifying emotions that shimmered through him.

She gave a tiny little sigh and snuggled deeper into the cushions. Though he was wary about even coming closer to her, he lifted one of the knit throws from the other sofa and spread it over her, tucking in the sides to keep out the draft.

In her sleep, the corners of her mouth tilted up slightly, but she didn't open her eyes.

He couldn't stand here all night, watching her sleep. Beyond the vaguely creepy, covert surveillance factor, it was Christmas Eve and he still had parental responsibilities.

He forced himself to move away from her and with all the stealth in his commando bag of tricks, he carefully climbed the stairs, avoiding any creaky steps. What would the other members of his team think if they knew he was using all his mad Ranger skills to check on a couple of girls who should be sleeping?

Did he care? Not really. The realization took him by surprise and he paused outside Tallie's room to let it soak in.

This might not be how he anticipated his life turning out. Fate could sometimes be a heartless bitch. Suzi and John certainly never expected to die in a plane crash before their youngest kid was even double digits. Emery never expected to lose her baby on Christmas Eve at the same time her bastard of a husband dumped all over her.

Life happened. Coming home to Idaho and becoming an instant father figure to two girls who needed him might not have been in the plan, but it wasn't bad, either. He needed to man up and stop acting like some kind of martyr who had sacrificed everything he wanted to take care of his sister's kids.

He was getting plenty back from the deal. He had the ranch and the girls and neighbors who cared about them, whether he wanted them to or not.

Not a bad trade at all.

And Emery. Where did she fit in?

He pushed that puzzle aside again while he checked Claire first and then Tallie. Unless they were putting on award-winning performances, both girls appeared sound asleep. He even called their names softly, but neither of them so much as stirred.

Satisfied they were genuinely asleep, he returned downstairs for the work ahead to find that Emery hadn't moved on the couch, either.

Apparently he was on his own for the whole Santa Claus thing.

Though he tried to be as quiet as possible, something must have awakened her. When he returned with the last armload of gifts from the SUV, he found her sitting up on the sofa, doing the finger-swipe thing over her eyes.

"Hey," she said, her voice low and rough from sleep. "Sorry. I didn't mean to conk out on you."

"No problem. If you're too tired for more holiday fun, don't worry about it. I can give you a lift back to your cabin and wrap things up here on my own."

"I'm fine." She yawned as she stood up. "Really, I'm fine. A little nap was all I needed and now I've got my second wind."

He wasn't convinced, but she proved her words by setting to work immediately.

She took the girls' stockings down from the mantel and filled them first and then began arranging the gifts under the tree.

Finally, she stepped back with a satisfied sigh. "It's perfect. Don't you think?"

"Absolutely," he answered, wondering if she sensed he was looking only at her, not at the room.

"The girls are going to have a wonderful Christmas morning. I only wish I could see their faces."

"Why can't you?"

Surprise and then discomfort flitted across her features. "I'm sorry. That wasn't a hint. I don't belong there, Nate. You've been kind enough to include me in some of your holiday celebrations, mostly because the girls insisted, but Christmas morning should be just for you and the girls. This is your chance to start some new traditions of your own with them."

He wanted to argue, but some part of him knew she was right. She would be gone in a few days, as difficult as that was for him to face. He and Tallie and Claire had to make their own way.

"Thank you, though, for letting me have a small part in your holiday," she said, her voice subdued. "If you want the truth, I've been dreading Christmas. Especially tonight. Christmas Eve, the anniversary of…the accident. This morning I was thinking I just wanted to sleep the day away and wake up about noon tomorrow. But I'm so glad I didn't. Tonight with the girls and with…with you has been wonderful. I'll never forget it."

He gazed at her in the multicolored light from the Christmas tree. Her sweep of blond hair reflected sparkles of red and gold and purple. All those tender emotions he had fought so hard against before returned stronger than ever and he couldn't help himself. He stepped forward and lowered his mouth to hers.

She sighed his name as he kissed her and her arms slid around his neck.

Now. *Now* the night felt perfect. Their kiss was slow and easy, like sinking into a soft bed at the end of a hard day.

Her mouth made him crazy. He thought he could spend forever just exploring every inch of those lips. He pulled her closer while the fire hummed and sparked behind them.

He wanted Emery Kendall more than any Christmas present he had ever wanted in his life put together. More than the official NFL leather football he'd begged and begged for when he was nine, more than the Element Fiberlight skateboard with the Independent trucks and the Bones wheels, more than the three-hundred-dollar twenty-year-old junker pickup truck he had bought himself for Christmas when he was seventeen.

He only wanted Emery.

But like the Ford Mustang he had *really* wanted that long-ago Christmas instead of a beat-up pickup truck, he suddenly realized he couldn't have this, couldn't have her.

What did he have to offer a woman like Emery Kendall except a faltering ranch and a couple of troubled, grieving little girls?

She was an elegant, sophisticated, country-club type

with her own design company, while he had barely graduated high school and just walked away from the only profession he had ever been good at.

Oh, she was attracted to him. A man could sense when a woman shivered at his touch, when she leaned into his kiss for more.

He could probably seduce her right here, right now—or better yet, take her up to his bedroom to spend Christmas Eve in her arms.

But in the morning, he didn't doubt they would both regret it. She was leaving in a few days, returning to her life in Virginia, and he couldn't afford to let this crazy tenderness inside him lead him to do or say something stupid that he couldn't take back.

He eased away from her, though it was just about the toughest thing he had ever had to do, and forced himself to rise from the sofa.

"You need some sleep. It's late and you have to be exhausted."

She blinked, her eyes a little dazed. "Not really."

He was fiercely tempted to take up the soft invitation in her eyes, but he couldn't do that to either of them.

"You will be if you don't get some sleep. Come on. I'll walk you back to your cabin."

For a moment, she looked as disoriented as if he had just hauled her over his shoulder, packed her outside and tossed her off the porch into the snow. But after a moment she nodded slowly, her expression veiled. "You're right. It's been a big day."

She said nothing more while she pulled her coat and scarf out of the closet and slipped them on.

"I can drive you if you're too cold to walk."

After a swift look, she focused again on knotting her scarf. "I'm fine walking. You don't need to come with me."

In answer, he only put on his coat and held the door open for her. The temperature had dropped a few more degrees in the short time since he had brought the presents into the house, but he barely felt the cold. He was aroused and frustrated and wondering if he had just made one of the biggest mistakes of his life.

They walked the short distance to her cabin, their boots crunching in the snow and their breath clouding out ahead of them.

"Thank you again for all your help," he said when they reached her cabin door.

She smiled, but it didn't quite reach her eyes. "You're welcome. I hope you and the girls have a wonderful day tomorrow."

"Today, you mean. It's past midnight. Merry Christmas."

She smiled a little, her gloved hands gripping the door-knob. "Same to you."

He wanted to kiss her again. To press her back against that door and then to push them both through it and shut out the world and all the differences between them. Instead, he forced himself to smile as if his heart wasn't dented and sore.

"Good night," he said, then turned and headed back through the snow toward the house.

She had to leave. After a sleepless night, Emery came to the bleak conclusion that staying at Hope Springs was only postponing her inevitable pain.

She rolled onto her back, gazing up at the now-familiar log beams overhead. That stunning, tender kiss the night before had only reinforced what she had begun to suspect days ago.

She was in love with Nate.

This wasn't merely infatuation or sexual attraction, though there was plenty of that zinging between them.

This was the real thing.

She was in love with Nate Cavazos, army Ranger, reluctant rancher, brand-new parent. She loved his strength and his awkward gentleness with his nieces and the deep core of honor and integrity that brought him back to his hometown to repay his debt to his sister by raising her children.

She was crazy about the man.

How could she have been so very foolish? Nate wasn't interested in a relationship. If he were, he wouldn't have pushed her away last night when it had to have been obvious to him how very much she wanted to stay.

He had been pushing her away since she arrived. She could see that now. If he'd had his way, he would have barred the proverbial gate to her the very first night she showed up in the storm.

Maybe it would have been better all the way around if she had just turned around that night and headed for Jackson, as he had tried to convince her to do. At least then she could have spared herself the pain she knew waited for her back in her real life.

No. She couldn't regret it. Even though she feared her heart might never recover from this week in eastern Idaho, that part of it would always remain here, she couldn't be sorry. The time with Tallie and Claire had been priceless and she had to hope that her efforts might have helped ease their grief in some small way.

She sat up, looking out the window at the brilliant sunshine glistening off the snow. She needed to go now. Why postpone the inevitable? Every moment she spent here would make her leaving all that much more difficult. She didn't have a flight for two more days, but she would change her plans and find an earlier one.

Christmas Day itself was one of the slowest air travel days of the year. She remembered reading that somewhere.

As she slid from the bed, grabbed her toiletries and headed for the shower, she had to wonder just how far she would have to go next year to outrun the memories of her holiday here at Hope Springs.

Antarctica, maybe?

Or perhaps somewhere warm, like sub-Saharan Africa.

No matter where she fled, she had a feeling she was doomed for next year and each December 25 afterward to compare every Christmas to this one.

"Come on, Uncle Nate! The French toast is going to be cold by the time we get there."

Nate raised an eyebrow at Claire's bossy tone, but decided not to get on her case about it. The girl ought to think about a career as a drill sergeant. His own grizzled hardcase of a sergeant at Basic Training hadn't ridden him half as hard.

"I'm coming. Hold your horses." He paused and managed a smile. "Oh, yeah. I'm the one with the horses."

Both girls giggled at his lame joke, which he had to admit was one of the best things about being their guardian. They laughed even when he was being silly or stupid.

"I hope Emery likes it," Tallie said, gnawing her lip as she looked at the flat package he carried, covered in rather juvenile wrapping paper with grinning snowmen and penguins on it.

"I'm sure she will," he said.

The girls seemed to have had a good Christmas. Though they had all experienced moments of poignancy, even melancholy, about celebrating the holiday without John and Suzi, they had been excited about their gifts. Even now, they each wore one of the new sweaters Emery had picked out for them.

But from the moment they unwrapped the last present, their dark heads had been close together as they cooked up some scheme while he put together breakfast. They finally revealed to him as they ate their French toast that they had a present for Emery and could they take it to her, along with some breakfast?

He hadn't been able to come up with a good reason to refuse, so here they were. He carried the gift—a watercolor of the ranch, complete with horses in the foreground and the jagged mountains in the back.

They had given one very similar to him, along with a sweater they said Joanie had helped them pick out before she left and a box of his favorite kind of cherry chocolates.

Emery would probably love the picture, but he wasn't at all sure he wanted to be here. He didn't need a repeat appearance of all those terrifying emotions churning through his gut. After their awkward parting the night before, he imagined Emery wouldn't exactly be thrilled to see him, either.

"I'm going to knock," Tallie declared, racing ahead of them to scamper up the porch steps.

She answered the door a moment later and the slightly tousled woman who had awakened on his great room sofa last night was nowhere in evidence this morning. Now she looked sleek and elegant in gray wool slacks and a red sweater with her hair pulled back in that complicated twist thing and perfectly coordinating jewelry.

She looked as if she were preparing for a luncheon at some fancy club. Who dressed up like that just to spend Christmas Day alone?

Her gaze found him and something intense and unreadable flashed in her blue eyes for just a moment before she turned to the girls with a bright smile.

"Good morning! Merry Christmas to both of you. I was hoping I would see you today. How was your Christmas?"

"Cool," Tallie exclaimed. "We got a *ton* of clothes and earrings and a bunch of books. And I got a new bike with eighteen speeds since my old one is a little kid's bike."

"I got an iPod," Claire said. "Want to see?"

"Of course. Come in."

"We brought you breakfast," Claire announced. "It's French toast. We helped Uncle Nate make it from our mom's recipe and it's pretty good."

"I had four pieces," Tallie confided.

"Is that right?" Emery smiled faintly.

Claire held out the parcel in her arms. "We brought you a present."

Astonishment flickered in those eyes and then a soft delight that somehow made all those crazy feelings start zinging around inside him again.

"You did?"

Tallie nodded. "We started it even before you gave us the quilts. But then we really wanted to give you something."

"How wonderful!"

Nate held it out for her and after an awkward pause, she reached for it. Their fingers brushed as she took the gift and it was all he could do not to yank her against him. Instead, he leaned a hip against the kitchen table as he watched her take the gift and begin to carefully unwrap it.

When she had pushed the last bit of paper aside, she turned it over and gazed for a long moment at the painting without saying anything.

Her reaction was everything the girls might have wished. Her eyes filled with tears and she gave a shaky-looking smile. "Oh, it's beautiful. Absolutely wonderful."

"We painted it together," Tallie said proudly. "Claire did the horses and the house and I did the mountains. I'm really good at mountains. And this morning after we had breakfast, Uncle Nate found a frame for us in the attic and helped us put it in it."

"This is the perfect gift for me to remember my time here when I go home. Thank you so much."

There was a strange note of finality in her voice and he wondered if either of the girls noticed. They didn't look very thrilled at the reminder that Emery's visit was temporary, but they didn't say anything, especially after she reached out and pulled them both into a hug.

"The picture will be priceless to me because you made it."

"There's a surprise in it," Tallie announced in a voice that, for her, sounded almost shy. "Can you see it?"

Emery studied the painting, her head tilted to the side as if she were standing in some fancy froufrou art gallery. She studied it for a long moment and then to Nate's surprise, her eyes filled up with tears.

"Oh, sweetheart," she murmured and pulled Tallie into a big hug.

Nate frowned. He hadn't seen anything unusual when he'd helped the girls frame it and now he craned his neck to see what all the fuss was about, to no avail.

"What is it?"

Emery pointed to a vee in Tallie's mountain peaks and

he finally saw it, a small figure camouflaged by a couple of dark green pine trees. He looked closer and realized the figure had wings and a little gold-crayon halo.

Tallie, Little Ms. Doubter who wouldn't even make an angel sugar cookie out of her defiance and anger, had drawn a tiny guardian angel looking over the ranch.

A lump swelled in his throat and he cleared it a couple of times before he spoke. Even then, his voice sounded a little on the ragged side. "Nice," he said.

Emery might not have wings or a halo, but she had been an angel to them, he realized. She had helped them through what could have been a very emotionally charged time, had given them all faith that things would get better.

He owed her more than he could ever repay.

"I have the perfect place in my townhouse to put it, right above my desk. That way I can look at it every day and remember our wonderful Christmas together," she said.

He hated thinking about her leaving. About how empty the ranch would feel without her.

"We're going to go see Noël," Claire said. "Would you like to come with us?"

Emery was clearly not dressed for traipsing through the barn, but she nodded. "I'd love it. Let me grab my coat."

She moved to the hanger by the door and suddenly Nate had a clear view through her bedroom door…to the suitcase open on the bed and the case holding her sewing machine that sat beside it.

She was leaving. Not in a few days, but now, today. He suddenly realized what had seemed off to him in her cabin. All the personal little touches she had brought to her living space these past few days were nowhere in evidence, all packed away for her return to Virginia.

Panic clawed at him, raw and intense, and for a long moment, he couldn't think what to do, what to say.

He could say nothing in front of the girls, so he blurted out the first thing that came to his head.

"You girls go on ahead," Nate said. "We'll be along in a minute, okay? I need to talk to Emery."

Tallie and Claire exchanged curious glances, but shrugged. "Okay," Claire said. "Can we give Annabelle some sugar?"

"Sure thing," he said. "But not too much."

They left in a clatter of pink boots and Nate closed the door behind them, then turned to face Emery, who was watching him with a hint of apprehension on her features.

"You're leaving."

The blunt words hung in the air between them, harsh and unadorned.

"Yes." She lifted her chin.

"I thought you weren't flying out for a few more days."

"I decided to see if I can catch an earlier flight."

Which was stronger? he wondered. The hurt or the regret or that panic that still squawked through him like static on a badly tuned radio?

"Why? What's the big rush?"

She didn't meet his gaze as she busied herself tying her scarf, something she did when she needed to keep her hands busy, he realized. "I have work waiting for me back in Warrenton. I finished several projects while I was here, but everything is piling up."

Bull, he wanted to say. *You're running away.*

But why shouldn't she? He had given her no indication she should stay.

"Is that the only reason you're taking off?"

She flashed him a quick look, then reached to pick up a pile of magazines from the coffee table.

"What other reason would I have?"

He said nothing, consumed by the grim knowledge that everything would be colorless and bleak when she left.

"Don't…" *Go* he almost said, but the words tangled in his throat.

"Don't what?" she asked, an arrested look in her eyes.

He couldn't beg her to stay, even as the words tangled together in his throat. All those differences still remained between them, a deep, wide chasm he didn't have the first idea how to cross.

"Don't forget these things."

He picked up a stack of books from the end table and handed them out to her, then froze, his attention arrested by the top item. It wasn't a book, he saw now. It was a photograph in a dated wood frame. He pulled the picture off the stack and held it up so he could examine it more closely.

"What the hell is this?"

"Nothing. Just an old photograph." She reached for it, but he held it just out of her reach.

The French toast he'd eaten for Christmas breakfast with the girls seemed to have suddenly congealed into a hard, greasy knot in his gut. "Why do you have a picture of Hank Dalton? And who's the woman?"

He looked closer at the picture and he knew. Suddenly he knew. She looked very much like Emery, with the same high cheekbones and classical features, though her clothes and hairstyle were several decades out of date, and the stunning truth slammed into him like a runaway bull.

"This woman is your mother, isn't she?"

She nodded shortly, looking vaguely sick herself.

"Hank Dalton is your father. The married man you were talking about."

Chapter Fourteen

He couldn't take it in. The woman he had come to... His mind shied away from the word he wanted to use and replaced in his head. The woman he had come to *care about* shared blood with the man he despised.

"Apparently." Though her features looked distressed, she spoke calmly. "I don't have any real proof, but that's what my mother said and she would have no reason to lie. She was in Jackson Hole on a tour with some girlfriends and met him at a bar. He swept her off her feet. Wined and dined her for a week, never mentioning his wife or his three sons who lived just on the other side of the mountains."

Three sons. Wade, Jake and Seth Dalton were her half brothers.

Suddenly everything made a twisted kind of sense. Her tension every time Wade Dalton came around, her strange reaction to Wade *and* Jake at the McRavens' party.

She'd come here to meet them. That was the reason she had picked Hope Springs to spend Christmas, because of its proximity to the Cold Creek Land & Cattle Company.

An accident of geography. Not fate, not destiny. He was an idiot not to have figured it all out.

"Why didn't you tell me?" His voice sounded harsh, strangled.

Tiny lines furrowed between her eyebrows. "I did. The other night I told you I only recently found out my mother was pregnant with me several months before she married Stephen Kendall."

"You didn't tell me you were a damn Dalton."

She swayed a little and her features looked pale suddenly above the bright red of her scarf. "I would appreciate it if you would keep this information to yourself," she said after a moment. "I've decided nothing will be gained by disrupting the lives of the Daltons. They don't need to know their father was unfaithful to their mother."

He gave a harsh laugh at that, then couldn't contain another and another. He sounded like a damn hyena, but he couldn't seem to stop. The whole town knew Hank Dalton was a lying, cheating son of a bitch. His sons had to know that better than anyone.

"I don't think it's going to come as much of a shock to anybody," he finally said. "You remember me telling you about the neighboring rancher my mother had an affair with? The man who ruined her life and cheated her out of land and money?"

She stared at him and her blue eyes—Dalton eyes, he realized now—looked huge in her pale features.

"Yep. Dear old dad. Your mother wasn't the first or the last and neither was mine."

She looked stricken, suddenly, and he didn't miss the way her hands trembled as she reached to take the photograph he finally handed out to her.

He was sorry suddenly that he had been so harsh. It wasn't her fault her father was Hank Dalton, the man he hated above all others.

"I guess it's a good thing I'm leaving today, then," she murmured.

"Yeah."

"Will you… Can you tell the girls I changed my mind about seeing Noël? Tell them I wasn't feeling good or something. It's not really a lie."

"You're not going to tell them goodbye yourself before you leave?"

She looked as if she would rather just slip away, but she finally nodded. "I'll find you all before I go."

He nodded and opened the door, wondering when he had ever felt so completely wrecked.

"Where's Emery?" Tallie immediately asked when he reached the barn a few moments later without her.

He offered the half-truth she had given him. "She wasn't feeling well. But I'm sure you'll see her later."

They both look disappointed and he screwed his eyes shut. They were going to be devastated when she left. Their whole Christmas would be ruined.

This was exactly what he had feared, the very reason he had wanted to keep her from them. Now they were going to have to suffer one more loss in their lives, a woman they had both come to love.

A woman they had *all* come to love.

He gazed at the tiny foal in the hay nuzzling up to her mother, their little Christmas miracle. The scene blurred in front of him and he blinked hard as the truth washed over him like a sandstorm.

He was in love with Emery.

Hopelessly, fiercely, irrevocably.

He drew in a ragged breath as all those well-reasoned arguments he'd been full of the night before crowded through his head. She was smart and sophisticated and beautiful. Nothing had changed. He still had nothing to offer her but a struggling ranch and a couple of orphaned girls who loved her.

So she was Hank Dalton's daughter. He couldn't blame her for her parentage anymore than he had any right to place the blame for their father's actions on the man's sons. Lord knows, his own mother wouldn't have exactly taken any prizes in the parenting department.

Tallie slipped a hand through his and he looked down to find her watching him with concern in her dark eyes.

"Are you okay, Uncle Nate?"

Far from it. He wanted to cry, for the first time since he was ten years old at his father's funeral.

"Yeah," he said, his voice gruff.

"I always get a little sad on Christmas day," Tallie confided in him.

"Why's that?"

"Because it's all almost over and we have to get back to real life. But don't worry, we can have an even better Christmas next year. We'll make tamales again and decorate the Christmas tree and maybe we'll even have two foals then."

He gazed at the motes of dust floating in a sunbeam like gold flakes from a glittery garland, a lump in his throat. Tallie was wrong. Next year wouldn't be better. Without

Emery, nothing would be. The thought of life on the ranch without her smiles and her gentleness and her kisses stretched out ahead of him, long and empty and miserable.

He straightened from the pen railing, his pulse pounding and determination uncoiling in his gut.

He couldn't let her go. At least not without trying to convince her to stay.

She refused to cry.

Though the emotions swelled up inside her in a hot, angry rush, Emery choked them all back, focusing only on gathering up the last of her belongings and stuffing them into the suitcase. She didn't care that she was wrinkling everything as she wadded and shoved and crammed.

She had to get out of here. Everywhere she looked were memories. Waking up the night of the blizzard to find Nate at her door. The tree where she and the girls had snipped evergreen boughs to decorate the house. The other cabin she could see through the window, where she had shared secrets and wrapped presents and kissed him until she couldn't hold two thoughts together.

And the girls. How was she ever going to get through saying goodbye to the girls? Just the thought of it had her fighting down a sob. She could hold it together for a few more moments, she told herself. She would be warm and casual with them and promise she would e-mail them after she returned to Warrenton.

Already her arms felt achy and empty, but she managed to hold on to her emotions as she began loading up the rented SUV. She left the food she'd purchased and the boxes of their parents' clothing she hadn't used in the quilts, but took everything else that belonged to her.

Finally the only thing she had left to load into the SUV was her largest suitcase. After one final sweep of the cabin, she rolled it out to the porch then bumped it down the steps. At the SUV, she reached to lift it with both hands, but it seemed as heavy as her heart. She wrestled it for a moment, pouring every ounce of her remaining strength into getting it off the snow-packed ground.

"Let me get that for you."

She froze at Nate's voice and prayed that the tears burning behind her eyes would just hang on for a few more moments.

"I've got it," she said stiffly.

"Do you?"

In that moment as he stood watching her trying to lift the heavy suitcase with that blasted unreadable expression, she hated him more than she had ever hated anyone or anything.

She hated him almost as much as she loved him.

"Go away, Nate. I can handle this."

He ignored her and reached for the suitcase with one hand. But instead of placing it in the cargo area of the SUV, he lifted it back up the steps and set it on the porch.

"Hey! What are you doing? I need that!" she exclaimed, following after him.

"I'll load it in a minute."

He made no move to explain himself, only stood on the porch looking down at her.

"Where are the girls?" she asked. Better that she could get this all out of the way now instead of having to drag out the goodbyes.

"They're still busy with Noël."

She was beginning to squirm under the intensity of that look, especially when he didn't say anything else. Could he see the desolation ripping through her when she thought about driving under the Hope Springs arch and leaving this place forever?

"If you will load up my suitcase," she finally said, hating that he was forcing her to ask, "I'll be on my way, out of your hair. You won't have to tolerate one of the terrible Daltons on your ranch another moment."

"Em."

She had been doing her best to avoid his gaze, but at the single word, she couldn't help it. She looked up and caught her breath at the expression in his eyes, dark and almost tortured.

"Don't," he murmured. Just that, nothing else.

Her heart gave one hard thump, then another and another. "Don't what?"

"Don't go. The girls want you to stay for Christmas dinner. I already put a ham in."

She curled her gloved hands into fists, furious suddenly that he was putting her through this. She couldn't keep up with him. One moment he looked at her with disgust, the next with that heat in his eyes she was helpless to resist.

"This is hard enough. Can't you see that? Please just give me my suitcase so I can go." She hated the small, distressed note in her voice, but couldn't seem to clear it away.

"Is that what you want?"

"You hate me because my father was Hank Dalton. I can understand that."

He shook his head. "I don't hate you. How could I?"

Finally, after far too much effort trying to contain them, one of the tears slipped through her defenses. In horror, she felt it slide down the side of her nose and she wiped at it with a violent gesture.

She heard Nate give a muffled groan and then an instant later, before she could even take a breath, he crossed the space between them and wrenched her into his arms.

"I don't hate you, Em," he repeated with stunning ferocity. "Far, far from it."

While she was still reeling from that, he kissed her with a softness and a sweetness that belied the intensity of his words and she didn't know what to do, what to say. She could only hold tight to his sweater with all her strength, afraid her knees would give out if she dared let go.

"Don't leave, Em. Stay, please. I'm sorry about earlier. About the way I acted. I was surprised, that's all. Will you stay? The girls would love it if you'd stay for Christmas."

A fledgling hope began to unfurl its tiny wings inside her, but she was afraid to give it room to soar yet. She could feel Nate's heartbeat under her fingertips and as she met his gaze again, she caught her breath at the emotions there.

"Wh-what about you?"

He was silent for a long moment, and then he smiled, something he did entirely too rarely. "I would love it if you'd stay much, much longer."

A wary sort of joy burst through her, but she was afraid to believe, after the misery of the past night and then this morning, and despite her best efforts to contain them, she could feel another tear slip through.

At the sight of it, Nate lifted his thumb and wiped it away and then he cupped her face in both hands.

"This is harder for me than anything I ever had to do in the army, and I've had to do some pretty tough things. But I'm going to come right out and say it. I'm in love with you, Em."

She stared, certain she must not have heard him right. "You're…what?"

"I think I fell hard for you the moment you walked in from the storm with your perky little hats and your complicated scarves and all the secrets in those Dalton eyes."

He kissed her again, his mouth warm in the cold Christmas air, and finally, finally, she let that hope begin to spread its wings.

"I know things are a mess here," he said. "But they're getting better, Em. I promise. I'm learning my way and figuring it all out. I don't have much to offer you, except a couple of girls who adore you and need you and a man who's crazy in love with you."

He paused, his gaze locked on hers. "The one thing I know for sure is that everything seems easier—better—when you're here, and it will kill me if you walk away. Please don't go."

In all her life, no one had ever said anything like that to her, had made her feel so very much wanted and needed. *This* was what she had been looking for when she came to Pine Gulch, she realized. Not her birth father's family. But this place.

This man.

This was good. It was right. It was every Christmas joy she had ever dreamed about magnified a million times.

She drew in a shuddering breath and then another one and then she flung her arms tightly around his neck and kissed him, laughing and crying at the same time, pouring everything she never thought she would have the chance to say into the embrace.

He made a rough, jubilant sort of sound and returned the kiss. When he pulled away several moments later, his eyes were dazed.

"I love you. Oh, Nate. I've been so miserable. It was devastating me to leave. I kept thinking this is the only place in my entire life that I've ever truly felt I belonged."

With that sexy groaning sound, he kissed her again, pushing her back into the cabin where it was a little warmer. And soon she was *much* warmer as he pulled her against his hard strength and deepened the kiss, his mouth hot and hungry on hers.

"Ewww."

Those girls and their impeccable timing again. Nate whispered an oath at the sound of Tallie's disgusted exclamation, but Emery only laughed against his mouth. She turned to find both girls standing in the doorway. Tallie's nose wrinkled at their embrace, but Claire's attention was fixed on the suitcase, her expression dark and troubled.

"You're leaving," she said in a betrayed sort of tone.

Emery opened her mouth to answer, but Nate beat her to it.

"She was going to. But I talked her out of it," he assured her niece. She looked as if she didn't believe him for a moment, then she tilted her head, taking in their embrace with first surprise and then a cautious hope.

"Is that true?" she demanded of Emery. "Are you staying?"

"I thought I would stick around for a while. Do you mind very much?"

Tallie squealed her approval and rushed to wrap her arms around both of them, but Claire still held back.

"How long is a while?" she asked.

Emery met Nate's gaze and smiled then turned back to his oldest niece. "I don't know. If it's okay with you all, I was thinking maybe forever."

Claire let out a small relieved laugh then joined them all in the embrace, and this time, as she was wrapped in the arms of their love, Emery didn't bother to hold back her tears.

Later that night when the girls were finally in bed after an exhausting day of board games, horseback rides and happiness, Nate sat on the couch in the great room with the Christmas tree lights sparkling and a fire in the grate and the woman he loved in his arms.

All day, he hadn't been able to stop touching her, to make sure she was real and that she was really his. Now, finally, she was in his arms and he felt truly at peace for the first time since he was ten years old.

"You're going to have to tell them, you know. Your brothers."

She lifted her head from his chest to stare at him and he wanted to smack his head with his open palm for bringing up the damn Daltons, when what he really wanted to do was continue making out on the couch.

"What about Marjorie?" she asked. "I don't want to hurt her."

He gave a rueful laugh. "I think that woman is long past being hurt by anything Hank Dalton might have done twenty-seven years ago. She's a tough old bird. If you want my opinion, I think she'll be thrilled to find you and so will her boys. They're going to welcome you into their family quicker than a cricket in the chicken yard."

He thought of it, having the Daltons for brothers-in-law. Not that he was jumping his horses too early here, but he already knew what he wanted—this woman in his arms forever. He was willing to take her any way he could get her, even if that meant having three interfering older half brothers with the package.

He framed her face in his hands, still not quite believing that he had his own Christmas angel right here beside him. "The Daltons will love you almost as much as I do," he said. "How can they not?"

She gave him one of those soft, tender smiles that never failed to take his breath away and then she kissed him back.

Nate thought about life at the ranch before she came, how he and the girls had just been going through the motions, trying to make it from one day to the next. She had done the impossible. With her smile and her quilts and her sugar cookies, she had brought joy and laughter back into their lives.

He held her in his arms as the fire burned low in the grate and the lights of the Christmas tree flickered in the window.

Once more, there was hope at Hope Springs.

'THIS EVENING I'm flying to New York for two weeks,'
Jasim imparted with a casualness that made her heart sink
like a stone. 'That's why I had you brought here. I own this
apartment and you'll be comfortable here while I'm abroad.'

'I can afford my own accommodation although I may not
need it for long. I'll have another job by the time you
get back—'

Jasim released a slightly harsh laugh. 'There's no need for
you to look for another position. How would I ever see you?
Don't you understand what I'm offering you?'

Elinor stood very still. 'No, I must be incredibly thick
because I haven't quite worked out yet what you're offering
me....'

His charismatic smile slashed his lean dark visage.
'Naturally, I want to take care of you....'

'No, thanks.' Elinor forced a smile and mentally willed him not to demean her with some sordid proposition. 'The only man who will ever take *care* of me with my agreement will be my husband. I'm willing to wait for you to come back but I'm not willing to be kept by you. I'm a very independent woman and what I give, I give freely.'

Jasim frowned. 'You make it all sound so serious.'

'What happened between us last night left pure chaos in its wake. Right now, I don't know whether I'm on my head or my heels. I'll stay for a while because I have nowhere else to go in the short term. So maybe it's good that you'll be away for a while.'

Jasim pulled out his wallet to extract a card. 'My private number,' he told her, presenting her with it as though it was a precious gift, which indeed it was. Many women would have done just about anything to gain access to that direct hotline to him, but his staff guarded his privacy with scrupulous care.

Before he could close the wallet, his blood ran cold in his veins. How could he have made such a serious oversight? What if he had got her pregnant? He knew that an unplanned pregnancy would engulf his life like an avalanche, crush his freedom and suffocate him. He barely stilled a shudder at the threat of such an outcome and thought how ironic it was that what his older brother had longed and prayed for to secure the line to the throne should strike Jasim as an absolute disaster....

* * *

What will proud Prince Jasim do if Elinor is expecting his royal baby? Perhaps an arranged marriage is the only solution! But will Elinor agree? Find out in DESERT PRINCE, BRIDE OF INNOCENCE by Lynne Graham [#2884], available from Harlequin Presents® in January 2010.

New Year, New Man!

*For the perfect New Year's punch,
blend the following:*

- *One woman determined to find her inner vixen*
- *A notorious—and notoriously hot!—playboy*
- *A provocative New Year's Eve bash*
- *An impulsive kiss that leads to a night of explosive passion!*

When the clock hits midnight Claire Daniels
kisses the guy standing closest to her, but
the kiss doesn't end after the bells stop ringing....

Look for

Moonstruck

by *USA TODAY* bestselling author

JULIE KENNER

Available January

---

red-hot reads

www.eHarlequin.com

HB79518

REQUEST YOUR FREE BOOKS!

2 FREE NOVELS PLUS 2 FREE GIFTS!

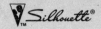

SPECIAL EDITION®

Life, Love and Family!

YES! Please send me 2 FREE Silhouette Special Edition® novels and my 2 FREE gifts (gifts are worth about $10). After receiving them, if I don't wish to receive any more books, I can return the shipping statement marked "cancel." If I don't cancel, I will receive 6 brand-new novels every month and be billed just $4.24 per book in the U.S. or $4.99 per book in Canada. That's a savings of at least 15% off the cover price! It's quite a bargain! Shipping and handling is just 50¢ per book.* I understand that accepting the 2 free books and gifts places me under no obligation to buy anything. I can always return a shipment and cancel at any time. Even if I never buy another book from Silhouette, the two free books and gifts are mine to keep forever.

235 SDN EYN4   335 SDN EYPG

Name	(PLEASE PRINT)
Address	Apt. #
City	State/Prov.	Zip/Postal Code

Signature (if under 18, a parent or guardian must sign)

Mail to the Silhouette Reader Service:
IN U.S.A.: P.O. Box 1867, Buffalo, NY 14240-1867
IN CANADA: P.O. Box 609, Fort Erie, Ontario L2A 5X3

Not valid to current subscribers of Silhouette Special Edition books.

Want to try two free books from another line?
Call 1-800-873-8635 or visit www.morefreebooks.com.

* Terms and prices subject to change without notice. Prices do not include applicable taxes. Sales tax applicable in N.Y. Canadian residents will be charged applicable provincial taxes and GST. Offer not valid in Quebec. This offer is limited to one order per household. All orders subject to approval. Credit or debit balances in a customer's account(s) may be offset by any other outstanding balance owed by or to the customer. Please allow 4 to 6 weeks for delivery. Offer available while quantities last.

Your Privacy: Silhouette is committed to protecting your privacy. Our Privacy Policy is available online at www.eHarlequin.com or upon request from the Reader Service. From time to time we make our lists of customers available to reputable third parties who may have a product or service of interest to you. If you would prefer we not share your name and address, please check here. ☐

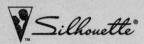

COMING NEXT MONTH
Available December 29, 2009

#2017 PRESCRIPTION FOR ROMANCE—Marie Ferrarella
The Baby Chase
Dr. Paul Armstrong had a funny feeling about Ramona Tate, the beautiful new PR manager for his famous fertility clinic. Was she a spy trying to uncover the institute's secrets…or a well-intentioned ingenue trying to steal his very heart?

#2018 BRANDED WITH HIS BABY—Stella Bagwell
Men of the West
Private nurse Maura Donovan had sworn off men—until she was trapped in close quarters during a freak thunderstorm with her patient's irresistible grandson Quint Cantrell. One thing led to another, and now she was pregnant with the rich rancher's baby!

#2019 LOVE AND THE SINGLE DAD—Susan Crosby
The McCoys of Chance City
On a rare visit to his hometown, photojournalist Donovan McCoy discovered he was the father of a young son. But the newly minted single dad wouldn't be single for long, if family law attorney—and former Chance City beauty queen—Laura Bannister had anything to say about it.

#2020 THE BACHELOR'S NORTHBRIDGE BRIDE—Victoria Pade
Northbridge Nuptials
Prim redhead Kate Perry knew thrill seeker Ry Grayson spelled trouble. It was a case of the unstoppable bachelor colliding with the unmovable bachelorette. But did the undeniable attraction between them suggest there were some Northbridge Nuptials in their near future?

#2021 THE ENGAGEMENT PROJECT—Brenda Harlen
Brides & Babies
Gage Richmond was a love-'em-and-leave-'em type—until his CEO dad demanded he settle down or miss out on a promotion. Now it was time to see if beautiful research scientist Megan Rourke would pose as Gage's fake fiancée…and if their feelings would stay fake for long.

#2022 THE SHERIFF'S SECRET WIFE—Christyne Butler
Bartender Racy Dillon didn't expect to run into her hometown nemesis, Sheriff Gage Steele, in Vegas—let alone marry him in a moment of abandon! Now they were headed back to their small town with a big secret…but was there more to this whiplash wedding than met the eye?

SSECNMBPA1209